World Without Love

Reunion

Book Two

Jaye Frances

World Without Love: Reunion - Book Two

Redstone Press Media

ISBN 978-0692625293

Printed in the United States of America

www.JayeFrances.com

A Note From the Author . . .

Reunion is the second book in the *World Without Love* series. The series is a continuing story and is meant to be read in sequence, beginning with Book One, *Betrayed*, available in kindle eBook and paperback from Amazon.

The *World Without Love* series contains mature content and is intended for an 18+ audience.

Even in hell,
there are rules . . .

Chapter One

It came to me slowly . . . I was no longer in the water.

Although I was fairly certain the mattress underneath me was real, I needed to touch something solid, to confirm this wasn't another hallucination.

I stopped myself just in time.

Until I was sure of the situation, I would remain dead-still, my eyes closed, listening for the subtle draw of someone's breath, the crack of a stiff joint, or the rustle of fabric from a shifting leg. My captivity on the *Kelsey* had taught me the value of concealing both my intentions and actions.

My brain was muddled from the beating I'd taken during the storm, but this much was a safe assumption: Someone had fished me out of the ocean. They had brought me aboard their boat and laid me in this bed. I had no idea how long I'd been here, if the time was measured in hours or days. My appetite should have given me a clue, but I wasn't hungry. Just tired and sore.

Forcing myself to lie there, feigning sleep, I listened . . .

The throb of diesel engines mixed with the sound of waves sloshing against the hull. Overhead, the constant footfalls from the deck indicated two, maybe three crewmen. In my mind's eye, I could see them stomping about in their high-topped, neoprene boots, the distinctive heavy thud of thick rubber on grooved teak suggesting this was a working boat, possibly a fishing trawler.

The last time I'd regained consciousness on a strange ship, I awoke in searing pain, shackled to a makeshift rack and half-covered in freezing water. This time, my discomfort was far less severe—the cramp of aching muscles and the sting from a minor laceration on my shoulder.

I counted to sixty. Then again, to be safe. I wouldn't make the mistake of opening my eyes too soon.

I moved a finger, swiping it across the scratchy cotton sheet. If someone was watching me, they didn't see it. Maybe I really was alone in the cabin.

I shifted my right arm. I wasn't bound. Whoever found me didn't consider me a threat. But I wasn't ready to make the same assumption about my rescuers. After what I'd been through, no one—at least in this part of the world—would ever again receive the benefit of the doubt. For all I knew there *could* be someone a few feet away, waiting for me to regain consciousness—someone really good at keeping their presence a secret.

There was no point in continuing to pretend I was asleep. Whether it was now or later, I would soon come face-to-face with the men on this boat. A few minutes, one way or the other, wouldn't make any difference.

I opened my eyes enough to form a blurry image. Directly overhead, the upper berth of a bunk-bed covered me like the lid of a coffin. A twinge of claustrophobia tightened around my throat. I turned on my side to escape the smothering delusion and propped myself up on one elbow, surveying the space.

I was alone.

Although covered with a blanket, my clothing was gone. I was naked. But that didn't necessarily indicate sinister intent. My shorts and top had been soaked with sea water, and removing them would have been the first step in raising my core temperature.

Needing a better view of my surroundings, I rolled on to my stomach. The movement forced me to stifle a moan—a reflex from the pain of shifting my weight from one part of my bruised body to another.

The cabin was tiny, not much larger than a handicapped bathroom stall. It made my assumption about the type of vessel even more likely. Small quarters were typical of the fifty to seventy foot class of trawler, where berth space was sacrificed for a larger cargo hold to maximize the volume of fish that could be stored during a single run.

I sat up, searching for clues. The more I could find out about my rescuers, the greater my initial advantage.

The small St. Christopher's medal hanging from a wall-peg brought a vague sense of relief. It was a real stretch of logic, but I doubted someone who was part of the slaver's network would be a regular church-goer.

Scanning the bulkhead behind me, I saw a faded picture of a pretty young woman with dark hair and large brown eyes. Below the photo, several plastic covered certificates reflected past safety inspections, fishing permits, and the boat's registration.

I needed to see more.

Rolling out of bed slowly, I hoped my movements suggested a nonthreatening rise to my feet, in case someone was watching from an adjacent or hidden part of the cabin.

Inside a small closet, I found a waterproof satchel containing a fold of Burmese currency, a driver's license, and a government ID from the Provence of Ayeyarwady. So far, I'd seen nothing to suggest the men on the deck above were anything more than local fishermen extending the benevolent efforts of a Good Samaritan.

Any remaining hesitancy over meeting my rescuers face-to-face was dispelled by the discovery of an English textbook. Opening the cover, I found a rubber stamp imprint—*Botata 4 High School*—and below it, *Property of Logan Morrison*. The hand-inked date under the name confirmed the book was two years old.

I tried to put it all together. The boat's captain was a family man with a son named Logan and a pretty, dark-haired wife, who was no doubt waiting at home, ready to greet him with food and affection after returning from a long day on the water. I was projecting a bit—even guessing. But I needed a break, and there was no better time for the universe to reverse my previous string of bad luck.

I had to find some clothes. Rummaging through the closet yielded a brown flannel shirt that fit me like a tent. I also found a pair of equally large denim jeans. I threw on the top and tied it to make it more manageable. But the pants presented a different problem. I could roll up the legs, but I had nothing to hold up the waist.

It was a challenge I never had to deal with.

Underneath the jeans, I'd noticed a neatly folded bundle of faded blue terrycloth. Thinking it was a large towel, I'd dismissed it. But with the pants no longer an option, I took another look. Opening it revealed a woman's robe. Immediately, I knew it was *hers*, kept on the boat for those rare occasions when she joined her husband for a shopping excursion or some personal business requiring an overnight stay in a neighboring harbor.

I had already tossed the shirt on the bed and was cinching the robe's ties around my waist when I wondered if the captain would mind me wearing it.

I decided it would give us something in common—his wife's robe; my need to use it.

Chapter Two

"The boat I was on capsized in the storm."

I brought the mug of hot tea close to my lips, not drinking, just letting the steam lick my face.

"What was her name?"

"Um, the Brighton . . . I think."

My save came too late. I could see the sudden suspicion on his face. The wisdom of trying to hide my escape from a slave ship was questionable at best.

"Any other survivors?"

"None that I know of. The storm came on fast. The first wave put the ship on its side. There was a lot of confusion. Most of the crew were washed overboard or trapped below deck. I tried to get to a life raft, but the boat began to sink. I managed to hang on to a piece of wreckage."

I'm offering too much information. Keep it simple and straightforward.

"You were lucky." His British accent colored his perfect English. "The storm took everyone by surprise. Lots of boats are still missing. Search parties won't be back until tonight. Then we'll know for sure."

We were standing inside the wheelhouse of a sixty-foot trawler. The boat was older, but its condition was immaculate. From the captain's chair to the original woodwork, every inch had been painstakingly restored to original condition. The only exception was the control station. Retrofitted with digital displays, depth finder, and a small radar screen, this boat was no factory vessel—it reflected the care of its proud owner.

Although I had no doubt this was Morrison—from the last name and picture on the driver's license I'd found while rummaging through the cabin—I kept waiting for him to confirm it. Not that he seemed reluctant to disclose his identity. He struck me as being quiet and not prone to small-talk.

I knew one thing for certain. Fishing was his livelihood. His boat, a single crewman, and a deck covered in nets and trap cages made it clear this was his business—and his life. Based on his muscular build and sea-worn face, I estimated him to be late forties. His full head of close-cropped reddish hair was beginning to gray, fitting him to a tee.

On the water since daybreak, he'd been plying his trawler through the storm's calm aftermath, taking advantage of the current-churned water—and the abundance of fish it often contained. He told me he'd spotted the drifting wreckage an hour after sunrise. Floating about three miles offshore, he'd noticed nothing remarkable about it at first—another piece of debris riding low in the swells.

His sighting of my unconscious body was as lucky as it was unlikely. A glint of gold—my blonde hair catching the sun at just the right angle—had made him curious enough to bring his boat closer and take a second look.

As he briefly described maneuvering alongside the broken remains of the *Kelsey*, I vaguely remembered the sound of an idling diesel and the cavitation of the prop. But I had no recollection of being brought onboard. Based on what Morrison told me, that had been nine hours ago.

I tried to recall the time I'd spent on the water after climbing onto the scrap of the *Kelsey's* hull. But my only memories were a confused jumble of determined breathing, struggling to keep my head above water, and desperately wishing I could relieve the ache in my arms and legs.

"From your lack of accent, I'd guess you're American."

I nodded. "San Diego, originally."

I waited for it, the question of what I was doing so far from home. Either he didn't care or wanted me to volunteer it.

"Unless you need a doctor," he said, "I'll take you to the police station in Yangon. They can arrange for the American consulate to verify your citizenship."

I held my palms up in a show of empty hands. "I lost everything, including my passport." I tightened the robe around me and brought the collar up, not out of modesty, but in response to the sudden bite of chilly, late-afternoon air.

"Then it's a matter of your family confirming your identity and paying for your passage back to the States."

I didn't disagree, deciding to keep my lack of family a secret. Instead, I asked, "Where are we . . . exactly?"

"On the southern coast of Burma. My family and I live in a small village called Mawdwin."

Outside, a young man tapped on the glass and gave the thumbs up, indicating the nets were out of the water.

"Your son?"

"Yes, that's Logan. He's with me fulltime now."

Logan Morrison appeared born to sail. Tanned and fit, he moved about the deck with strength and grace, every muscle in his body responding in perfect symmetry to the motion of the boat. With strong cheekbones, dark eyes, and burnished-brown hair, it was obvious he'd inherited most of his features from his mother. Based on the date in the textbook, I estimated him to be about twenty.

His father pushed the throttle forward, the bow of the boat rising in response to the throaty growl from the engines. They were headed home, and I was finally getting off the ocean.

Fifteen minutes later, the coastline gave way to a small, natural harbor.

"Is that where you live?" I pointed toward the distant collection of vessels, and beyond, to the modest homes scattered across the hills. I felt like I was dragging information out of him, but I wanted to hear some regular chit-chat about hometowns and family, because it sounded good, and familiar—and safe.

Morrison nodded. "Mawdwin's an old fishing village. As far as I know, it's been there forever."

"And the photograph of the dark-haired woman in the cabin, that's your wife?"

He smiled. "Yes, that's my Maria. That picture was taken years ago, but she's still just as beautiful."

I felt the uneasy tension between us subsiding. He was beginning to relax, his grip on the controls not quite as firm. I looked back to the stern, where Logan was busy freeing the last of the squirming fish from the twisted mesh of net.

"And your son . . . he works with you every day?"

"I had hoped he would go to university or learn a trade that would keep him off the water. But the last four years he's spent most of his free time helping me run this boat, giving up his weekends while he was in school. Now he tells me fishing is all he wants to do." Morrison paused. "I won't force him to give it up."

He seemed sincere, honest.

I made the decision on the spot. I had to trust someone. Morrison had saved my life. That should count for something.

I started slowly. "I haven't told you everything about the boat I was on . . . and why I was on it."

Until now, Morrison had rarely suspended his focus from the horizon, and then only to check a gauge on the engine panel. Seeing him pull back on the throttle and reduce our speed to half thickened the air with an invisible layer of tension.

Shifting his weight, he looked at me . . . waiting.

I hesitated, not sure how to begin. Was I making a mistake? Morrison had rescued me from the surface of the ocean, and now I was going to tell him I was an escaped sex slave, running from thugs and criminals who wouldn't hesitate to harm him if he got in their way. Not exactly the best way to express my gratitude.

I could see Morrison's impatience beginning to build. Not wanting to irritate him further, I blurted it out, eliminating the possibility of changing my mind mid-sentence. "The ship I was on, it wasn't the *Brighton*. It was the *Kelsey*. And I wasn't a passenger, not in the usual sense. I was a prisoner. The captain was taking me to an auction, to be sold as a sex slave. If the storm hadn't swamped the boat, I'd already be someone's property, being forced to do God knows what."

Deep furrows crept across Morrison's brow. I wondered if he was becoming suspicious or was just plain worried. Maybe he was thinking of his family, keeping them safe, especially if he knew about the network of slavers—the kind of men who would go to any lengths to reclaim their property. He was probably wishing he'd never seen me clinging to that water-soaked section of planking, debating whether to throw me back in the water, because someone like me was far too dangerous to have on his boat.

"There's a good chance the captain didn't survive," I continued. "As far as I know there was only one member of the crew who made it through the storm."

"One is all it takes." Morrison looked back toward the horizon. I could tell he was thinking, weighing the odds, considering his options. "That man . . . do you know where he is, what happened to him?"

"I'm pretty sure he's aboard the *Kochi Mar.* They spotted our life raft and turned their ship toward us. That was before I decided to slip over the side."

"You went into the water intentionally during the storm?" He was looking at me as if I were a ghost, an apparition that could fade away at any moment.

"I wouldn't let them take me. Not again."

Morrison fell quiet, his mouth grinding in silence, chewing on his thoughts. Finally he said, "I don't know either boat, not by name or reputation. 'Course, we don't get much commercial traffic this far off the regular trade routes. But I've heard the stories, about kidnapping young girls, selling them to the highest bidder. Nasty business."

I'd been holding my breath, not sure how Morrison would respond. I let it out gradually, trying to control my sudden need for air.

"I can't take you into town," he continued. "Not in the daylight. There's a chance they're already looking for you. A light-skinned blonde girl will draw too much attention. People will ask questions."

There was concern in his voice, but not panic, his words carrying the measured, unhurried tone of a man who wasn't easily bluffed.

"You'll have to stay out of sight until I can determine the best way to get you to the American embassy in Rangoon." He paused, letting his voice build with challenge. "How did you get tangled up with slavers?"

I knew the truth would make me sound like some kind of tramp. But he deserved to know. My presence on his boat could easily put him and his family in jeopardy, and I wasn't going to keep anything from him. "My husband gave me up to pay a debt. He lost me . . . in a card game."

So far, Morrison had shown guarded concern over my predicament. Now his eyes narrowed in incredulous disbelief. "How could something like that happen? How could *you* let it happen?"

It was a fair question. I'd already wondered how different things might be if I'd disappeared out the back door while the men were playing poker. But it was too late to second-guess my lack of responsible judgment. The best I could do was separate my circumstances from my identity, convince Morrison I was an innocent victim, and my association with the lowest dregs of humanity was the result of force, not choice.

"I know what you must be thinking," I began. "If you keep company with criminals, you start picking up their habits. But it wasn't like that. The men who took me were strangers. My husband had just met them. Neither of us had any idea who they were. They started playing cards and my husband got in over his head. Maybe he panicked or got scared."

I could tell he wasn't convinced. I also knew there was little I could do to change his mind. I only hoped he had enough compassion to recognize I desperately needed help.

He fixed his gaze on my face in the same way a parent locks eyes with a wayward child. "It's not my place to pass judgment. I never met your husband, but it seems to me if a man would do that to his wife—bet her in a card game—well, you should have seen it coming a long time ago."

I nodded, acknowledging what he'd said. I wasn't going to offer excuses or try to defend myself. I couldn't take the risk of alienating the only man who could help me. I would let him talk, say what was on his mind.

The silence was suddenly awkward. He was waiting for me to respond. I lowered my head, more comfortable with the clean field of faded teak than with Morrison's piercing eyes.

"We met while he was in the Navy. I was a couple of years out of high school. I thought he really loved me."

Morrison stroked his chin. "You're young, and what brought you to this part of the world is none of my business. But this isn't some peaceful suburb in the States. There's not much law here, and what little there is can't be trusted. A young, pretty girl like you can easily find herself at the mercy of people who would think nothing of turning her out for sex, or for that matter, putting a bullet in her head."

His words were harsh, his voice strict, but there was something else—an underlying concern that told me he was beginning to understand. I felt a guarded sense of relief, a reprieve from rejection.

I needed to sit. The only place in the wheelhouse was the top of a storage bin built into the back wall. Without saying anything, I stepped backward and plopped myself down, pulling my knees up tight against my chest. I looked up at Morrison, hoping he could see the saddest set of eyes I could muster.

"Alright, you've got yourself in a jam and you need help. You can stay with my wife and I until you hear from the embassy." There was caution in his voice, but the worry on his face was gone. "I won't be able to use a land-line to contact them, or even a cell phone. Too many ears. I'll have to find a secure email link on a government website, a way to contact the state department. Otherwise, it's going to take some time."

Except for the low pulsing drone from the engines and the occasional thump from the coils of rope hitting the deck where Logan worked at the stern, the small wheelhouse was suddenly quiet.

Realizing our conversation was over, I said, "Thanks. It means a lot to me." I knew there was more I should say, but I was empty. I buried my head and for the first time, let the tears come.

I was finally on my way home.

Chapter Three

Morrison had increased speed. Arriving in the small port before the other boats would mean fewer eyes—and questions—as we moved from the dock to his truck. But as we entered the mouth of the harbor, I could see over half the slips were full, and a number of larger boats were setting anchor.

"We'll wait until sunset to head in," Morrison said. "It'll be safer after dark."

Lingering in the swells a thousand yards from the dock was unusual, and crewmembers from other boats often waved as they passed, many of them asking if Morrison needed help. "Nope, all good," he would shout back. "Just cleaning the traps before I take her in."

An hour later, he guided his boat through the fading twilight, approaching the vacant slip with plodding caution. As Logan secured the lines, I pressed against the window of the wheelhouse, looking out at the maze of floating wharfs and docking berths. A few held larger boats, like Morrison's. Most accommodated fifty-foot trawlers or converted pleasure craft, all equipped for small-trade fishing. Back-lit by the dusky sky, the forest of radar-masts, outrigging, and deck booms rose from the graying shadows like the ash-black ruins of some lost and forgotten civilization.

"Move away from the window," Morrison barked. "Your blonde hair is a dead giveaway."

I jumped back. "Sorry, I'm not thinking."

He switched off the bridge lights. "Here, put this on." He handed me a dark gray rain slicker. "It will help disguise your shape. And there's a pair of boots on the deck."

As I brought the hood over my head, Morrison frowned. "It looks suspicious, like you're trying to hide under all that rubber."

"What if I got wet, and need to stay warm?"

"No, it'll draw attention. And keep the front of the coat open, loose."

"How do I hide my hair?"

"Use this." He plopped a cap on my head. "I'll get a bedroll from the cabin. Carry it on your left shoulder, between your face and the marina. I'll stay on your right."

His plan was simple. In the event someone approached us, he would pretend to have forgotten something on the boat and send me back for it.

It seemed like we were leaving a lot to chance.

Seeing how nervous I was, he tried to reassure me. "There's no moon. I doubt anyone will notice you. You'll be fine."

With Logan staying behind to lock down the boat, we walked toward the dirt-covered parking lot. Morrison responded to several men also leaving the docks, their distance not a threat to my identity. The exchanges were pleasant and quick, with only one asking about Morrison's "new hand."

"Where's Logan? Did you get yourself a replacement?"

Without breaking stride, Morrison answered. "He's making sure the batteries are charged for tomorrow. This is Michael, my wife's nephew. He thought he wanted to learn to fish. But after spending a day on the water, I think he's changed his mind."

The other men laughed, offered a wave, and continued walking.

We hiked the remaining distance to the parking lot unchallenged. Morrison threw the bedroll into the back of his short-bed pick-up, started the engine, and shifted into reverse.

"Aren't we going to wait for Logan?"

"He likes to sleep on the boat. Makes him feel independent, like he has his own place."

I'd expected to have Logan with us. Not only for the ride, but later on as well. While I didn't have any reason to be suspicious of Morrison, his son's presence in the house would keep him honest, and less tempted by the occasional stray thought.

The road was littered with gravel-filled potholes and broken sections of pavement. Although the ride was uncomfortable, the bounce and vibration provided a reasonable substitute for conversation. I was hesitant to ask Morrison any more questions. I didn't want to come across as nosy or prying—I felt like I'd volunteered enough information. If he wanted to know more, he could ask. We completed the fifteen minute trip with only the sounds from the washboard road filling the silence.

I assumed our destination was one of the small two-bedroom flats lining the road or one of the run-down apartment buildings, their parking lots strewn with abandoned cars and piles of flattened cardboard boxes. Instead, we turned down a narrow, private driveway prominently marked with the Morrison name and address.

I'd had no indication—other than the comparatively superior size of his boat—that Morrison's financial status was anything other than the typical family fishing operation, scraping by on just enough money to keep his family fed. Finding the Morrison home to be a charming two-story stone chalet with a wide front porch and large windows flanked with louvered shutters was surprising.

A few outdoor floods revealed strategically placed trees and a well-manicured flower garden—more promises that the rising sun would reveal an enchanted cottage taken from the pages of a child's storybook.

"You can get out here and wait for me on the porch. I'll park the truck around back."

I hopped out, taking care not to slam the door. I didn't want to broadcast our arrival to Morrison's wife. I knew he hadn't called ahead to let her know he was bringing home a guest. 'Too many ears,' he'd said.

As I waited at the front of the house, I pulled off the rain slicker and dropped it across the porch railing, then slipped off the rubber boots.

Standing on that porch, looking up at the star-splattered sky filled me with a sense of relief. Morrison and his son were the only people who knew I was alive. Soon, Morrison's wife, Maria, would also know.

Three people . . . none of them slavers.

I could worry about it tomorrow. But not tonight. Tonight I was free. And all I wanted to do was scrub myself clean and sleep in a real bed.

I heard Morrison's boots crunching into the footpath gravel, approaching from the side of the house. I waited for him to join me on the porch. "Should I stay outside until you've had a chance to talk to your wife?"

He shook his head. "Maria's not like that." He opened the front door and ushered me inside.

The relative luxury of the Morrison home continued throughout its interior. At my feet, a faux-marble tile floor reflected the gleam from two overhead mica-quartz lighting fixtures, the bound glass shades washing the room with the warm hues of the setting sun. An open-beamed ceiling soared at least twenty feet, spanning a second story walkway and loft. At the end of the room, a huge fieldstone fireplace offset any hint of opulence with its warm, cozy presence.

The scent of baking bread and cinnamon washed over me like new hope. For a moment, it took me back to my mom's kitchen during the holidays, when she spent most of the afternoon preparing a huge meal for the three of us.

As my bare feet touched the tile, I thought how ragged I must look. Here was Morrison, bringing home some stray urchin he'd found floating in the sea. Oh, and by the way, she's also a runaway sex slave with a price on her head.

I wasn't sure how he would handle that. But if I understood Morrison correctly, it would never come up.

"Maria, this is Jewel. The boat she was on capsized and broke up in last night's storm."

From the faded condition—and obvious age—of the photograph I'd seen on the boat, I'd expected the hands of time to have set a wrinkle or two across her brow. But my first impression of Maria completely dispelled the idea of an aging housewife. Silky, shoulder-length hair framed a flawless face, and her smooth, olive–bronze skin glowed from the sun's kiss. A sense of genuine warmth radiated from her sparkling, chestnut eyes, and her inviting smile dismissed any suggestion of pretense. While she was clearly older than the young woman in the picture, her face and body reflected a fortuitous combination of genetics and healthy lifestyle.

Without hesitating, she rushed to greet me, wrapping her arms around me in a friendly hug. I felt it immediately—there was an ease about her, a gentle and welcoming acceptance that dismissed any sense of intrusion.

"It's a miracle your husband found me," I said, wanting Morrison to hear. "If he hadn't come along when he did, I would still be out there, floating on a piece of wreckage." I'd done a lousy job of thanking her husband and I wanted him to understand I was truly grateful.

"You poor thing." She pulled me tighter, gently caressing my back through the worn terrycloth. "Well, he *did* find you, and that's all that matters. We'll get some food into you, and after a good night's sleep, you'll feel a hundred times better." She turned toward her husband. "Pauly Morrison, you didn't have anything onboard for Jewel to wear except my old robe?"

"No, no," I stammered, intercepting the question. "It's not his fault. I'm afraid I put it on without asking."

Maria stepped back and quickly scanned me from head-to-toe. "We're close enough in size. Let's go upstairs and see what we can find." She turned to Morrison. "Logan's staying on the boat tonight?"

"Told me he wanted to."

"Then Jewel can use his room."

As I followed Maria upstairs, I was impressed with her youthful energy. She was probably mid-forties, but it didn't matter. She was simply a beautiful woman who cast a happy shadow on everyone around her.

"Sit on the bed," Maria said as we entered the master bedroom. She opened the middle drawer of a triple dresser and pulled out a pink sleeveless blouse. "Try this. It might be a bit tight around the chest, but it should fit the rest of you fine." I held the top against me, smoothing out the wrinkles. She brought her hands to the fabric, pinning it against my breasts.

It could have been awkward, even uncomfortable.

It wasn't.

Returning to the dresser, she pulled out several pairs of shorts and tossed them on the bed. "You'll have to try these on. They're all the same size, but each one fits a bit different. I seldom wear them anymore. And when I do, it's just around the house, never in town. Pauly says they're too revealing. Especially for a woman with a son as old as Logan."

I wanted to argue with her, tell her how flat her stomach was, how the draw of her waist was in perfect symmetry to the outward curve of her bottom. Instead, I thanked her for the clothes.

"I'll get you some shampoo and conditioner." She disappeared into the bathroom.

Taking it as an invitation, I followed her in.

The bath sparkled, not only from consistent, regimental cleaning, but also from its modern design and use of materials. Double sinks equally divided the six-foot granite vanity, while the wall-to-wall mirror reflected the large glass-block walk-in shower. The colors of the sea were everywhere—in the blue-gray ceramic tile, the pale green glass trim inlays, and the oyster-white lighting fixtures. More a personal spa than bathroom, its level of luxury and extravagance was in stark contrast to the simple, rudimentary buildings and small, unpainted structures I'd noticed on the drive from the harbor.

"Step inside the shower," she said. "If you'd like, I'll wash your hair for you. The ocean can strip the life out of it, so it's best to leave the conditioner in a bit longer than usual."

I hadn't expected her to stay, but I didn't argue. I slipped out of the salty-damp robe and let it fall to the floor.

She reached for the valve handle and turned on the water. "It takes a minute to warm up. But there's plenty of it."

"Maria, I know this is none of my business, but your home, this bathroom, it's something right out of a magazine. How did you manage to find the materials, the contractors, the . . ." I stopped, realizing I was being too nosy.

"The money?" she asked.

I felt my cheeks flush bright red. "No, that's not what I meant."

She laughed. "Let me assure you, our fishing business is not that good. Oh, it makes enough to pay the bills. But this house? We inherited it from my parents."

I nodded, relieved that Maria had glossed over my rude curiosity.

"My father built it as a gift for my mother," she continued. "As a teenager, my mom had always wanted to live in a large, beautiful city on the coast. She dreamed of looking out at the water from a luxury high-rise apartment." She paused and smiled, her gold-flecked eyes sparkling with memories. "My mother grew up in poverty, and she wanted a life high above the violence and fear she'd witnessed on the streets. But my father's work kept him here in the village. So instead, he built this home for her. I've always wondered if it made her just as happy. If not, she kept it well hidden."

Maria's voice was as soft and soothing as the water pouring over me. And yet, I was trembling. The spray from the shower—the sudden surge of warmth—had reactivated my senses, confirming my body was still here, in one piece, despite the sea's best attempts to end my life.

Without thinking, I reached out, needing to connect with the living.

Maria instinctively took my hands in hers. "Don't worry," she whispered. "You're safe now."

I shut my eyes, wishing I could pull her close.

She must have sensed it.

I felt her arms closing around me, her soft breasts pressing against mine. I should have been concerned about her clothes, about the liberties I was taking with someone I had just met. But my thoughts were elsewhere. With our bodies touching, my hands confirmed the soft nape of her neck, the gentle curve of her back.

Annie!

Dear God, what was I doing?

For a moment, Annie had come back to me—if only in spirit. I could open my eyes and destroy the fantasy, or I could keep her with me for another few seconds.

I couldn't bear to do either.

Dropping my head on Maria's shoulder, I broke into shuddering sobs. Without hesitating, she cradled me as if I were a lost child, bringing her cheek against mine.

For the longest time, she held me, gently stroking my hair, her lips lightly brushing against my cheek. Standing there, in the safety of her arms, her touch was more effective—more healing—than a year's worth of therapy.

She waited for my tears to stop, for my breathing to calm into slow, steady draws. "I need to take this top off. I'm soaked." She said it matter-of-fact, without a hint of teasing innuendo—simply an explanation of what she was going to do, perhaps to make *me* feel comfortable.

I felt embarrassed. "You don't have to stay. I can finish."

"I don't mind," she reassured me. "But if you'd rather be alone, I understand."

"I don't know what I want," I whispered.

She smiled. "Give me a second."

I felt the separation as she stepped away from me. For a moment, I lifted my face into the spray, trying to hide it.

By the time I turned back to Maria, she had unbuttoned her blouse and tossed it on the vanity. Her reflected image from the misted mirror gave the artificial sense of seeing her at a distance, and I gazed at her the way a weary traveler finally lays eyes on their home town.

Her breasts were round and full, her dark nipples in perfect proportion and size. Peeling off her skirt, she let it drop to the floor. I wondered about her husband, if there was a chance he might come upstairs to check on us.

I chased the thought from my mind.

Maria turned on the second shower head and removed it from its cradle. "Tilt your head back." Cupping her hand at the top of my brow, she sprayed my hair.

As her fingers brought the shampoo to my scalp, I felt the caress of someone warm and caring.

Touching me.

"Close your eyes." She rinsed the suds, catching some in her hand to clean my shoulders. "You're going to have a few bruises here. I have some vitamin E lotion. It will help."

Replacing the shower head, Maria directed the spray to the side. Lathering the soap, she spread it over my skin. Unlike the cautious approach of an indifferent caregiver, her hands glided over me with unfettered abandon. As she worked her way down my back, I realized I was inching closer, subtly asking her to continue.

"I can't imagine what it must have been like out there in the dark, alone in the storm."

She paused at the dimples at the top of my butt, hesitating.

My heart dropped as I realized she might be finished.

Feeling her soapy fingers begin to circle my bottom set off a steady exhale—I didn't want her to know how much her nurturing hands were affecting me.

Not yet.

"The sea can really damage your skin," she continued. "But you avoided the worst of it. It's the salt in combination with the sun that dries it out."

I knew I should be making conversation, asking about her life, her family. But I had immersed myself in the lingering contact of her hands on my hips, and the gentle, unhurried brush of her fingertips across my stomach. Maria was a balm for my senses, repairing more than the destructive effects of the elements.

She fumbled with the soap as she set it on the ledge. She was finished, ready to leave. I reached back and found her free hand. "Do you have to go?" My voice sounded needy. My actions confirmed it.

The flow from the second shower valve stopped. "I'm just turning off the water. I don't want my hair to get all wet." She dropped to one knee. "I'll use the shampoo. It's not as harsh as the bar soap."

Maybe she *had* been ready to leave and changed her mind, accommodating me out of concern for what I'd been through. In a way that was neither selfish nor insensitive, I didn't care. She had returned to me, reconnecting with both hands. Starting at my ankles, she worked her way up my legs, taking her time as she washed my thighs.

I let go of any hesitation, any concern that I was being too brash, too forward. I inched backward, separating my feet. My movements were impossible to misinterpret, yet they seemed natural, instinctive.

As Maria worked her way between my legs, her fingers brushed the outer folds of my vagina, intentionally avoiding full contact.

I was done being coy. I'd been through hell, and a big part of me was still out there, adrift on the ocean. I leaned forward and placed my hands on the shower wall. I wanted to give her access to every inch of me, to join with me in a way that would confirm I was human—and alive.

Hearing my breath quicken was not enough to convince her I was ready for more. She waited until my soft moans came free and unrestrained, my shameless whispers of encouragement a testament to how much I needed this.

She did not tease me, nor did she rush our union. She seemed to intuitively understand that under different circumstances, without the trials of the last three days, I would not have been so desperate for another's embrace. Even the fact it was her—a woman I had met only an hour ago—could easily be interpreted as convenience rather than choice. But from what I could tell, none of that mattered to Maria. It was as if she had been waiting for me, in this house, ready to give me back my soul.

Maria's fingers continued to follow my natural crevices, lingering over both openings, gently circling without entering.

"Is this okay?" she asked.

"Yes, it feels good." I ached to turn to her, to hold her close and press my breasts against hers. But we were devoted strangers, committed to playing our parts—she giving, me receiving.

I didn't dare move.

I released a spontaneous sigh of pleasure.

Maria took it as a sign. She began pausing at both openings, each time letting the tip of a single finger penetrate a little deeper.

Half an hour ago, she was a kind and generous woman, inviting me into her home, extending simple hospitality. Now she offered pleasure and distraction–without expectation. I didn't question her reasons. For all I knew, she could be an angelic surrogate for the Saints, her actions motivated by mercy . . . even pity.

I didn't care. Her selfless affection was displacing the memory of the last twenty-four hours, helping me forget how close I'd come to dying.

Sensing my rising pleasure, Maria continued, pushing me to the edge, teasing my ass with one finger while gently massaging my clit with another. I wished I had her in front of me, able to see, touch, and taste her.

My orgasm came in a series of deep, breath-grabbing contractions.

"Let it go," she whispered. "Let it flow out of you."

Finally able to face her, I pulled her in. I was ruining her hair, but I wanted more. She was the source of safety and warmth surging through me, and I needed to bond with her.

Gently placing my lips over hers, I saturated her mouth with wet kisses. She happily responded, parting her lips, inviting me to explore with my tongue.

I began stroking her bare back, caressing her skin as if reuniting with an old lover.

Annie's face flashed in front of my eyes.

I had dismissed it the first time, rationalizing her ethereal presence as a symptom of exhaustion and stress. But now, the thought haunted me. Was I using the innocent affections of a stranger to keep my grief at bay? Was Maria nothing more than a convenient reincarnation of my precious Annie?

It was selfish, and unfair . . . and worse, deliberate.

But I had to let it go. Weighing the right or wrong of it was pointless. I could no more push Annie from my thoughts than I could deny the pleasure of holding Maria's naked body against mine. Annie's memory would always be a part of me, and I would carry her with me for the rest of my life.

Maria and I were sharing this moment without any thought of tomorrow. She had not asked for a place in my heart. Her gifts of affection came from compassion and kindness, not from promises of devotion.

I nudged Maria from the shower. With closed eyes, and guided only by the soft fibers of the thick bath rug under our feet, we shuffled with careful, cautious steps. I was unwilling to break my sacred union with her, even if only to glance for obstacles that waited in the unfamiliar space.

Reaching the vanity, Maria leaned back, inviting me to wander over her wet, slick skin. Never letting my hands—or my mouth— disengage from her, I nestled against her glistening breasts, moving from one nipple to the other, covering them with my lips, drawing them in. The symbolism was impossible to escape—in so many ways, she was returning me to the living, giving me the opportunity to *feel* again.

I was reluctant to leave them, but the rest of her body was waiting.

Dropping to my knees, I drew large wet circles on her stomach with my tongue as my hands explored the curve of her bottom and the firm, muscular tone of her thighs. Converging on her smooth, hairless mound, I found the tiny crease that defined the start of her moist lips—waiting to be kissed. Without hesitating, I licked her from top to bottom, brushing her clit with my tongue, tasting her juices, wanting more.

Marie's fingers played over my shoulders, fondling the back of my head, caressing my hair.

If I *was* transferring my grief for Annie into a living substitute, I couldn't have chosen a more satisfying—or beautiful—one.

"I haven't felt the touch of a woman in so long." Maria was breathless, on the edge. "I'd forgotten how much I—"

The shockwave of orgasm tore through her, every muscle in her body pulsing in spasms of release. I stayed with her, extending my tongue deep into her passage, holding it there until I was sure she was ready to part from me.

Standing to face her, I wrapped my arms around her and kissed her. Maria nuzzled against my neck, the vanilla scent of her damp hair filling my nostrils. In no hurry to separate, we lingered in the solitude of the moist, steamy bath.

Maybe a shrink would have a better way of articulating what had just happened, describing it as a healing experience or a therapeutic cleansing of the spirit. But I didn't need to rationalize our actions with authoritative jargon. I only knew how much better—more human—I felt. Maria possessed the rare gift of empathy, of intuitively knowing my needs. Willing to give of herself, she had reached out to me in a way that went far beyond the physical, forming the intimate connection I so desperately needed.

"It's getting chilly," Maria said. "Let's dry off. I'll get you a clean robe from the closet. That old one from the boat is nearly threadbare."

She glanced in the mirror. "God, I'm a mess. And I have to go to the store before dinner."

"You want me to go with you?" I said it without thinking, forgetting the risk of leaving the house. Morrison had brought me in wearing an old gray rain slicker—an impromptu disguise to avoid dangerous attention. And he'd done it for a reason. "You know," I added, "now that I think about it, I'd rather lie down for a bit before dinner."

"You might want to take a nap," Maria suggested. "I'll wake you when I get back. You can help me throw together a salad."

"I'd like that, Ann—" I caught myself, hoping I'd done it in time.

"And what?" Maria asked.

"Nothing. I was just thinking how good a salad would taste."

With the passion of the moment passing, I couldn't help but see the similarities. It was uncanny how much she reminded me of Annie, perhaps of who she would have become in twenty years. Even so, I told myself to be more careful. I couldn't allow another slip of the tongue to betray Maria's trust.

Dressing quickly, and unconcerned about her wet hair, Maria started for the door. Before leaving, she turned and looked back at me. "I won't be long. If you need something, you'll find Pauly in the garage getting ready for tomorrow. Logan's room is at the end of the hall. Make yourself at home."

She blew me a kiss as she left.

Two doors away, Logan's room was small compared to the master. Furnished with a double bed, dresser, and a single nightstand, it seemed spartan for a young man. Under different circumstances, it might have felt cramped. But tonight, it was more comfortable than the finest hotel room.

For the first time in a nearly a week, I felt safe.

Chapter Four

"What part of the States are you from?"

Finally, a question I could answer truthfully.

"California."

"Isn't that where all the movie stars live?"

"A lot of them do." I was always amazed at the fascination the rest of the world had with American actors and music icons, often equating their status to that of European royalty.

"They have something in the air there. They call it smog," Paul added.

"Something they put in on purpose? To make it better?" Maria turned pensive, but I could tell she was pretending, playing the patsy to her husband's baiting.

Paul smiled. "Yes, dear. They pump it into the sky, to turn the sunset red."

"You're making fun of me," she scolded. "You shouldn't do that in front of our guest."

"Smog comes from car exhaust. It's a kind of pollution," I said. I knew their banter was good-natured kidding. But I wanted it clear I was on Maria's side.

"I think it's because the people who live there are always driving somewhere," Maria added.

I thought for a moment. "Yes, I suppose that's true."

"I remember reading an article about how people in California drive their cars with no real destination. Can you imagine it, Pauly? Driving the road for the pure enjoyment of it?"

He shook his head. "The day I don't have to spend another minute behind the wheel of that truck can't come soon enough."

"It's actually gotten better," I said. "The smog, I mean. There's less now than ten years ago." I felt the pangs of homesickness. The sooner I was on a plane headed for San Diego, the better.

"Can I get you anything else?" Maria was on her feet, headed toward the kitchen.

"No, thank you, everything's perfect." And it was.

Dinner had been pleasant and informal. At first, I'd felt the uncomfortable sense of being a third wheel, knowing I was imposing on what would otherwise be a time of intimate conversation between Maria and Paul. But both seemed truly pleased I had joined them.

Especially Maria.

She'd sat close, punctuating every question and comment with a touch. Often letting her hand linger, she occasionally offered a gentle squeeze before letting go.

Paul paid little attention to his wife's flirtatious behavior. He either didn't care or had seen it before and knew it was simply an innocent exchange between two women.

I wondered if he would feel the same way if he knew how much Maria and I had enjoyed each other a couple of hours earlier. I wondered if she'd tell him.

Chapter Five

"They put you in my room?"

I'd left the bedroom door cracked. As it swept open, I'd assumed it was Maria coming in to check on me.

I recognized Logan right away.

"Yes," I whispered, propping myself up on one elbow. "Your dad thought you were staying on the boat. I didn't mean to take over your room. I'll be up and out in a minute. I can sleep on the couch downstairs."

"You don't need to move. I'm not staying. I only came back to get some clean clothes."

I realized he had an unrestricted view of my breasts. Hoping I hadn't embarrassed him, I pulled the covers up.

"It's okay," he grinned. "I've seen them before. I was the one who pulled you out of the ocean."

"I thought your father found me."

"He saw you floating. But I was the one who brought the dingy over and pulled you off that piece of scrap."

I heard the male vanity in his voice, wanting recognition.

"So you brought me back to the boat by yourself?"

He nodded. I was sure I saw him stand a little straighter.

"And I guess you were also the one who took my clothes off and put me in the bed?"

Even in the dim light from the hallway, I could see he was embarrassed.

"I should have thanked you earlier," I added, "for saving my life."

He shuffled from one foot to the other, seemingly uncomfortable with the praise.

"I must have looked like a drowned rat. I'd been on that broken section of the boat for—"

"No," he interrupted. "You looked so pretty . . . and helpless. I mean, I wasn't sure how to hold on to you, to lift you into the dingy." He paused. "I saw the bruises on your ankles. Did you get those from the wreck?"

"I got banged up when the boat capsized." There was no point in telling him the truth.

Even through the shadows, I saw his young face etched with sympathy. His reactions were so traditionally male, reflecting the appropriate concern over a woman's suffering. It was cute as hell.

I reached out in a spontaneous gesture, giving him permission to come closer. Intertwining his fingers with mine, I felt a surge of emotion sweep through me. Although he'd pulled me off the ocean hours ago, *this* was rescue—the heat of a man, his unspoken question lingering in the air between us.

On the *Kelsey,* I would have had to accommodate him whether I wanted to or not. Now I was being asked. Not with words, but with a caress. And what I said—what I decided—would be honored.

Another indication I was finally free.

I felt the quiver in his hand. He was nervous, perhaps not sure what to do next, or not sure what I *wanted* him to do.

I didn't need to think about it. The bed was cold and lonely. The thought of him lying next to me was intoxicating. He was so young, so delightfully vulnerable. That's what made him so right, and nonthreatening. Bursting with male libido, he would come to me, driven by the anticipation of exploring my body without restriction, by the thrill of plunging his cock inside me.

My reasons were not near as exciting.

Joining with him would be my way of re-establishing a connection between my body and mind—broken by the men of the *Kelsey*. Maria had started the process. I needed a man to complete it.

I swept back the covers. "Keep me warm?"

His face lit up like a fireworks display, his solid jawline offering a crooked smile while revealing straight, white teeth.

Quickly, quietly, he locked the door and removed his clothes. The sight of his firm, tight butt—the defined and toned muscles flexing as he walked in front of the bed—made me want to stop time. His broad shoulders emphasized his trim waist, and his unblemished honey-bronze skin glowed in the window's peeking light from a newly rising moon.

His cock was large, noticeably longer and with a much greater girth than my husband's. Unfettered by gravity, it stood proud and straight, and reminded me of the oversized genitals portrayed on Asian deities of fertility. It was the kind of penis my gay art teacher from high school would have called a 'magnificent symbol of manhood.'

I couldn't wait to put my hands on him.

I thought about Maria. Seducing her son would be a poor way to repay her kindness. Perhaps his father would understand, but Maria would not. She had invited me into her home, trusting me to be careful with her possessions. Although Logan was no longer a child, I was sure she considered him to be her most precious keepsake.

Logan sat on the edge of the bed. "I think I should apologize."

"I don't understand."

"On the boat, after I took off your clothes and laid you on the bunk . . ." He hesitated, suddenly uncomfortable.

"What's wrong, Logan?"

"I touched you. It was only for a second or two, but you were unconscious. I took advantage and I shouldn't have done it." He paused, then added, "I'm sorry."

I had forgotten the look of pure innocence.

"Show me," I said.

"What?"

"Show me how you touched me."

Even in the dusky moonlight, I could see his eyes were locked on mine, maybe in youthful fascination or to acquaint himself with the girl waiting for him in his bed. Without saying a word, he laid his hand on my hip and slid his fingers across the crack of my ass.

"Like that," he whispered.

I turned my head to one side, looking away. "I don't think I can forgive you."

His back straightened, his muscles tensing. "Why?" His voice cracked with desperation, concerned he'd done something inexcusable.

"There's nothing to forgive. You were gentle. You had no intention of hurting me. If I'd been awake, I wouldn't have stopped you. Just like I'm not stopping you now."

Tightening his grip on my butt told me his deliverance from past transgressions had been overshadowed by the excitement of future possibilities.

I patted the mattress. "Lie next to me."

He didn't hesitate.

I slid my hand across his shoulder as he moved close, letting him work through the initial awkwardness of joining with a stranger for the first time. Feeling a rush of pleasure as his engorged dick nestled against my belly, I waited for him to begin, thinking he would want to wander over my body in adolescent discovery.

But Logan's need was urgent. He was not interested in savoring the slow caress of my hand or the pleasure of my warm, slick tongue on his cock. His thoughts were focused on fucking me.

Settling between my legs, he placed the head of his dick against my pussy and pushed inside. Although I was wet and flowing, the sudden intrusion caused me to wince as my vagina stretched to accommodate his huge shaft.

His first few strokes were mechanical, pounding away at me the way a jackhammer attacks a block of concrete. It didn't last long. In seconds, the tremors in his torso told me he was on the edge of release.

"Slow down," I whispered. "No need to rush."

A constricted moan was all he could manage.

"Logan, listen to me. If you stop now, hold back, you can fuck me over and over again, for as long as you want."

He stopped mid-stroke, his face strained and dotted with tiny beads of sweat. He was desperately trying to control his building orgasm. But the overwhelming stimulation of joining his naked flesh with mine had honed every nerve in his rock-hard penis to razor-sharp intensity.

His expression etched in frenzied panic, he drew a deep breath in a final attempt to quell his raging urge to come.

Too late.

His liquid exploded deep inside me, his cock momentarily suspended in a blanket of hot jism.

His impulsive haste to fuck me was disappointing, but not surprising. Like many young men, he had yet to appreciate the delicious ache of teetering on the edge of orgasm, until the line between restraint and release became a blurred rush of pleasure, his final surrender leaving us exhausted, satisfied, and bathed in a gush of cum.

In time, he would learn the art of joining with a new lover. With experience, he would discover the decadent sensuality of running his fingertips over a woman's breasts to sense the quickening pace of her heart. As each new woman left her mark, he would come to appreciate the tangy bite of a sweat-coated belly as he drew his mouth toward the sweet nectar of her wet pussy. And when his boyish cravings finally ripened into passionate surrender, he would welcome the embrace of her trembling thighs as his lover's delicious anticipation exploded into waves of orgasmic delight.

That's why what he did next was so unexpected.

Withdrawing his cock, he slid lower, tracing my skin with his tongue. Again, his actions were quick, his destination seemingly more important than the journey.

Pausing below my belly, he pressed his face into the wet junction. Nuzzling close, his tongue darted in and out, swiping at the lips of my dripping pussy, and tasting—perhaps for the first time—the mix of juices. Covering the semen-soaked folds of my vagina with his mouth, his upper lip brushed against my clit.

My gasping squeal of delight was impossible to contain.

It was all he needed.

Without hesitation, he plunged his tongue deep, spreading the lips, drawing his cum—and mine—into his mouth.

Bringing my hands to the back of his head, I gathered tuffs of his hair between my fingers. I would not allow him to wander, to become distracted by an impulsive need to explore another part of my body. He could suck on my breasts later. He could slide his cock into my mouth *after* I'd come.

But not before.

His hands swept my chest, his gentle pinching and twisting of my swollen nipples forcing me to arch my back in abandon.

Captivated by his tongue, his mouth, his hungry lips, I was racing toward surrender.

Interpreting my rising torso as an invitation, Logan coated his fingers with our juices and slipped a single digit inside my smallest hole, then added a second. The combination was delicious—his fingers filling my ass, his soft tongue flicking over my clit.

Waves of silky heat flashed from the very center of our union.

Shaking uncontrollably, I felt the spark of an escalating howl. Afraid it would shatter the erotic silence, I let it escape as a series of broken whimpers.

I hoped his parents hadn't heard it.

Logan began to pull away.

It didn't matter. I couldn't take any more.

"Is everything . . ." He paused, looking concerned. And maybe a little scared. "I mean, are you okay?"

I'd forgotten how young he was—this might have been the first female orgasm he'd ever seen.

"Yesssss . . . I'm fine."

I pulled him up, wanting to taste his mouth.

He spoke before I could kiss him.

"I've got to go. If my parents find me in here . . ."

The risk of being discovered overruled his passion. His body satisfied, he was too distracted to stay with me.

He pulled back, his anxious expression an unspoken question—asking permission to leave. Craving a final embrace, I pulled him against me, laying his head on my chest, raking my fingers through his hair.

"Go," I said. "And leave the door cracked."

Without as much as a parting kiss on my cheek, he lifted off me, carefully shifting his legs across the bed. In less than a minute, he'd grabbed some clean clothes from the dresser and was ready to go.

Lifting his hand in an awkward gesture, he mouthed the word *Bye*.

I wasn't sure if he saw the wink I offered before he turned and tiptoed into the hall.

It didn't matter. That's not what he would remember about me. More likely, I would become that unexplainable smile that crossed his lips on some otherwise unremarkable day, when for no reason, his mind was stirred by the memory of an "older" woman who shared his bed in a moment of forbidden pleasure.

Chapter Six

For the last two days, Maria and I had been inseparable, alone in the house while Logan and his father pursued a rare migration of Spanish mackerel. Dancing around each other like school children, we spent most of the time in endless chatter—about her family, her background, our early loves and heartaches.

She had given me exactly what I needed—someone to talk to. Someone to listen.

With our conversation punctuated by frequent kisses and lingering hugs, we reveled in the process of getting to know each other. I hoped we were building a relationship that would survive my eventual disclosure of what had happened to me onboard the *Kelsey*.

I wanted to tell her everything—how my husband had put a price on my head, then bet and lost me in a card game. I wanted her to know what was going through my mind when the crew of the *Kelsey* stretched me out on the table and filled every one of my holes. I ached to share my grief with her, to tell her how close Annie and I had become in such a short time. I especially wanted to tell her how much she reminded me of my lost friend, how alike they were in spirit. And although I hated to admit it, I wanted to tell her how I'd imagined it was the captain standing on the sinking wheelhouse of the *Kelsey*—and not caring what happened to him.

Instead, I'd been careful, fabricating my answers with constructed detail, trying to remember what I was saying so I could repeat it, enlarge on it if she asked later. I hated lying to her, knowing she trusted me. But Paul Morrison had made it clear the first night I was in the house: 'I don't want my wife to know anything about the ship you were on, or what you were doing there. It's for your own good. I want you to promise you'll keep it to yourself.'

Knowing I shared secrets with her husband only made me feel worse. But I knew he was right. The fewer people who knew the truth meant less risk for those around me. *Knowing* was dangerous. But it didn't make it any easier—lying to Maria.

Before leaving on the extended fishing trip with Logan, Morrison had assured me he would contact the American consulate in Rangoon. 'I'll call on a public landline and use an alias,' he'd said. 'Safer that way, for both of us.'

I had naively thought Morrison's phone call would unleash a team of political and diplomatic forces that would not rest until I was safely repatriated. I even imagined a squad of U.S. Marines arriving at Morrison's front door, ready to whisk me away in a helicopter to the nearest American military base. But in reality, my return to the States would follow a road paved with many layers of bureaucratic red tape. First, my request for assistance would be forwarded to the State Department, where my name would be run through various databases and records. If everything checked out and they confirmed my status as an American citizen in distress, Thailand's government would be asked to assist with an immigration waiver. Along the way, my file would be shuffled from one in-basket to another, lying on someone's desk for God knows how long before it was finally approved. Morrison guessed the process could easily take the better part of thirty days.

Knowing I would have to wait another month before my country confirmed my identity and nationality was disappointing. But it was a start, and eventually I would receive the help I needed to return home.

I wondered if Morrison would allow me to share my real story with Maria—*after* he'd been assured my story was true. The choices that put me on the *Kelsey* were not my own. I was a victim of greed, and I needed to share the ugly details with someone who would understand. But I also knew that in this part of the world, vengeance often replaced justice. Grudges could last a lifetime, and retribution was not always swift. While I would return to a life of relative normalcy, Paul Morrison would continue to live under a shadow of doubt, always wondering if the stranger lurking on the next corner had been sent to extract revenge for helping me avoid recapture. It was a burden he would carry for the rest of his life.

In spite of the necessary deception, Maria's influence had worked its magic, reminding me I was worth more than a pile of poker chips. She was living proof I could still make something of my life, and this experience was simply an unfortunate detour I would soon put behind me.

"That was Pauly," Maria said, putting down her cell phone. "They're on the water. They have a good catch started and he doesn't want to bring the boat in until tonight. But he needs a part for the engine, some kind of electrical gadget. I need to pick it up at the marine supply and bring it to the dock. He's got someone waiting to ferry the part to him."

"Are they stranded on the water?"

"No, he said the boat's working fine. He's just being cautious. The hold is fully loaded with fish and he doesn't want to risk straining the engine. I'll change my clothes and we can get on the road. If you want, we can even have a quick lunch at the River View restaurant. They serve really great chicken curry."

I froze. "If it's okay, I think I'd like to stay here, maybe read a little."

"Are you sure? You haven't been out of the house in three days. The sun would be good for you."

I smiled and shook my head, hoping it would be enough. "I don't think I'm ready to be out in a crowd yet. It feels good to sit on the porch, look out at the flowers. I know that must sound crazy."

Maria smiled. "I should have realized you need some time alone. We've been together nearly every minute." Maria paused, and then added, "I've been acting like a love-struck teenager, for Christ's sake."

In many ways she was right. The last two nights we had slept in her bed. Cuddling close, we'd traded kisses and slow caresses, delighting in the warm sensation of our constant connection.

"*We've* been acting like love-struck teenagers," I corrected her. "And I've enjoyed every minute of it."

Maria giggled. "I promise I won't be gone for more than two hours. It's about a thirty-five minute drive each way, then another fifteen to the dock. But I can never count on the traffic."

"I'll be fine. Don't worry about me."

She grabbed her purse and started for the door. Immediately, I was behind her, pulling her back before she could turn the handle. It was more than passion that brought our lips together. After being kidnapped and subjected to the whims of sex-hungry men, I relished the exchange of real affection. While my tryst with Logan had reminded me of how enjoyable a man's body could be, it had been a spontaneous encounter, his young face and form a succulent piece of fruit from a forbidden part of the garden—a place where I could never return. On the other hand, Maria had been my savior. From the moment I walked into her home, she had welcomed me with an open heart, willing to share herself without questions or conditions. Even though she would be gone only a couple of hours, I would miss her.

Watching her slide behind the wheel of the tiny Japanese import, I waved at her through the kitchen window, then realized she couldn't see me through the glare of the glass.

Seeing her drive down the tree-shaded path onto the main road brought an unexpected—and uncomfortable—sense of isolation. It made me realize how much I wanted a life like hers—the security of a home, the joy of a family, the promise of a shared future.

While Maria had admitted the occasional pang of disappointment—as predictability replaced spontaneity in her relationship with her husband—she had assured me it was a better situation than always looking for something more exciting. 'That's the tradeoff,' she'd explained, 'giving up the promise of something new in exchange for stability, a sense of satisfaction in the permanence of a home, and having people in your life who truly care about you.'

Maria had been gone less than twenty minutes when I heard the snap of the front door latch.

She must have forgotten something. I glanced around for her purse. No, she'd had that with her when she left. Then I remembered the pair of sunglasses she always wore when venturing outside. I checked the counter next to the wine rack—their usual place. They were gone.

"Jewel?"

Paul Morrison's voice was unmistakable. Startled, I began buttoning the open blouse I'd thrown on before breakfast.

He wasn't supposed to be off the water until the end of the day. Something had brought him in early. It had to be mechanical problems. The part that he'd called about and asked Maria to pick up from town must have broken down completely.

"I'm in the kitchen," I called out. "I thought you were Maria. She left about twenty minutes ago, and—"

"I know," he interrupted, abruptly appearing in the doorway. "I saw her leave."

Morrison's appearance defied him having been on the water for two days. His clothes were clean, his face recently shaven. And there was something else. He seemed nervous, jumpy—not the same man I'd seen three days ago on the bridge of his boat as I'd explained my situation.

Wait a minute . . . *I saw her leave?* That made no sense.

I hesitated, suddenly uncomfortable. He hadn't seen his wife in over two days. Why didn't he stop her?

"There's someone here." Morrison cleared his throat. "He says he knows you."

It shot through me like leftover lightning from the storm. *Someone who knows me?* Had he brought an official from the embassy?

No, an embassy officer might know something *about* me, but they wouldn't know *me*.

My husband!

That had to be it. The bastard had tracked me down. Unable to deal with his own guilt and stupidity, he'd finally come to his senses, hoping I would forgive him. Okay, that was fine. I would use him as my way out. I would tell him what he wanted to hear, get my passport, and use his money to buy a plane ticket home.

Then he could rot in hell.

With Morrison standing in the doorway, I figured Carl was behind him, too ashamed to face me. He was probably waiting for me to make the first move.

"So where is he?" I asked. "Where's that excuse for a husband hiding?"

Having dismissed Morrison's obvious anxiety as symptoms from his role as the uncomfortable man in the middle, I waited to see the return of his usual, quiet confidence—as much a part of him as his rugged, weather-worn face. Instead, he was turning pale, glancing down at the floor as I brought my eyes to his.

Something was wrong.

"This man," he began, his voice strained. "He says he's a friend of yours. I ran into him on the dock. He wanted me to bring him right over."

Someone from the docks?

That didn't sound like Carl. He would never misrepresent himself.

Black and white. The bottom line. No bullshit. That was Carl.

So if it wasn't my husband, who was it? And more important, why would Morrison reveal my presence to anyone? He had insisted on secrecy, asking me to avoid all contact with the locals until he could—

"Hello, Jewel." The voice was familiar, but I couldn't quite place it, like trying to recognize a shadowy figure from a bad dream.

Someone was coming up behind Morrison.

Morrison stepped forward, allowing the other man to enter.

My breath caught in my chest. I was panting, my stomach threatening to heave. "NO . . . NO . . . NO!"

R.J. stepped into the room.

I had jumped into a raging ocean—and nearly died—to escape him. I was sure he thought I was dead, a victim of the storm. Now he was here, standing in front of me.

His face broke into a wide grin, a kind of I-told-you-so look that reconfirmed his self-assured arrogance. "Nice to see you, Jewel. For a while there, I thought we'd lost you."

Fear had a choke-hold on my throat. I forced out the words. "I'm not going back with you. Do you hear me? I'm not leaving this house."

"Now, Jewel," R.J. began, "you need to calm down. You know what can happen if you don't cooperate. So don't try anything stupid."

"You're the one who's being stupid," I snarled. "Get away from me, you piece of shit, or I'm going to call the police."

"Oh, I wouldn't do that. They're *already* looking for you. The captain put the word out two days ago. Fact of the matter is, there's not a safe place for you anywhere in this country—unless you're with me."

The captain. *Alive.*

I reached back, searching for the counter, needing a handhold. I wasn't sure which I would do first—faint or throw up.

"You owe Morrison here a big debt of thanks," R.J. continued. "He kept you hidden, off the streets until I could track you down."

I swallowed hard, determined to keep the contents of my stomach from rising into my throat. Finally, I looked squarely at Morrison. "Why?"

Again, his eyes swept the floor. Unable to face me, he turned to R.J. and spoke only to him. "Alright, I've done my part. Now get her out of her. And remember, half the reward, that's what you said."

"And that's what you'll get," R.J. assured him. "When she's back in the captain's hands."

You fucking bastard. I wanted to scream it in Morrison's face. I had trusted him, believing he would help me. Instead, he'd turned me in, keeping me in his home until he could collect a reward posted by the captain.

Morrison turned to R.J. "You bring some rope? I don't want you losing her on the road and cheating me out of what I got coming."

The combination of disbelief and shock was enough to send me to my knees. The anger, however, was another thing entirely. My body was pumping enough adrenalin to make me consider the odds of taking them both on. I told myself to wait, store it and use it later, when I had the advantage of surprise or a weapon within easy reach.

"What about Maria?" My voice was little more than a forced whisper.

"What about her?" Morrison responded, his voice edgy and defensive.

"Does she know?"

"She will, when the time is right."

He had purposely sent Maria on an invented errand to get her out of the house so she wouldn't see R.J. arrive to retrieve his lost "property." No doubt the two of them had waited down the street, approaching the house after seeing her leave for the city.

"How much?" I asked. Even though I could feel a sneer distorting my face, my expression revealed only a fraction of the revulsion I had for both of them.

Morrison looked at me with feigned confusion.

His contrived innocence infuriated me. "I'm talking to *you*, you fucking asshole. How much is R.J. paying you? How much did it take to buy your soul?"

"Get her out of here," Morrison hissed. "I don't want to take the chance of Logan seeing this."

"I thought you left him on the boat," R.J. said.

"I did, but I told him I was only going to be gone a few minutes. I don't want him finding us here."

Logan!

Without thinking, I unleashed the cruelest kind of hatred, the kind that doesn't discriminate between the innocent and the guilty. "You think you're protecting your son from the truth? You're too late."

"What are you talking about?" For the first time, I saw fear in Morrison's eyes.

"I fucked your precious little boy. Did you know that? Then he ate my pussy. That's right, I held his head tight against my pussy while he ate his own cum. Something you'll never be man enough to do. So you think about that, keep that picture in your mind when you all sit down to dinner tonight. Your boy, Logan, with his face pushed deep between my legs, slurping up the juice, loving every minute of it."

Even as the words left my mouth, I recoiled at what I'd said. I was trying to hurt Morrison, but it was a stupid move. The only thing I'd accomplished was to assure him he'd made the right decision, encouraging him to get this foul-mouthed slut out of his house.

A week ago, I would have been incapable of such a callous and vindictive attack. But my captivity on the *Kelsey* had changed me, my explosive outburst another indication of the rage that was building inside of me. Although it didn't excuse my behavior, my anger was becoming a kind of holy inspiration for what I would eventually do to these men.

Morrison's face flushed bright red. "Get her out of here, *now!* I don't want this bitch in my house another second." He was moments away from flying across the kitchen and trouncing me into the floor.

It had become so easy for Morrison to place the blame, to pronounce judgment, to separate himself from the guilty. I mentally added Morrison's name to *the list*, realizing there were now four men that needed killing.

Chapter Seven

R.J. clamped down on the cuffs a second time, forcing the ratchet to the next notch, the way an animal trap sets its jaws deep into quivering flesh. "You got one hell of a mouth on you, girl." He spun me around, forcing me to face him. "The first thing you're gonna learn is when to keep it shut, and we're starting your lessons right now."

Another lesson. Another excuse to torment me and force me into submission.

R.J. had moved first, pinning me against the counter, preventing me from opening a drawer and grabbing a knife. With Morrison blocking the kitchen doorway, there was no point in trying to resist. I'd never get past both of them.

I stood motionless as R.J. fastened a leather strap around my ankles, leaving enough slack to allow short steps. Adding a tether between my feet and the handcuffs, he created an effective leash to control my movements.

"You can't expect me to walk like this. And my wrists hurt like hell."

"The only thing I expect is for you to keep your fucking mouth shut." Lifting me off the ground like a sack of potatoes, R.J. threw me over his shoulder and started for the front door. "Watch your head." It was an afterthought at best, his voice carrying the hopeful expectation the top of the door jamb would leave a mark on my scalp.

As R.J. carried me outside, Morrison watched from the porch. From the grim determination on his face, I could tell he'd made peace with his conscience. For an instant, I entertained the idea he'd been afraid for Maria, worried about what might happen to her if the captain and his henchmen found out he had tried to help me escape. If that were true—if his motivations were born from fear— it might help buffer the overwhelming sense of betrayal I felt. But *betrayal* was too civilized a word. Human beings betrayed each other, with a kind of treachery that required an understanding of human dignity, a compromise of integrity, a breach of ethical touchstones. Morrison had made it clear his integrity was for sale.

Later, I would learn Morrison would lie to Maria, making up a story about my background and character, telling her I was a dangerous psychopath and the authorities had come for me. He would tell her it was best I was out of their lives, and she should forget I ever existed.

He had proven himself to be an imposter and hypocrite. In every sense, he was worse than a slaver. And as he stood on the porch of his inherited stone cottage, he was as transparent as an apathetic bystander watching a lynch mob drag an innocent victim to the gallows.

I desperately wanted to tell him . . . someday, when he least expected it, he would find me waiting, ready to repay him for his treachery.

Yet, as much as I despised him, he was my only link to Maria.

I called out to him. "Tell Maria I'm sorry. Tell her . . ." I stopped. I couldn't trust him to convey anything with accuracy. Someday, I would tell her the truth. And somehow, I would make her believe it.

R.J. had parked a cargo van by the side of the house, leaving the rear doors open. He sat me on the edge of the bumper.

"Roll in," he commanded.

The smell hit me like an iron fist—rotting fish and rancid cooking grease. The floor's wooden slats had been water-proofed with recycled fat obtained from restaurants. The black, sticky residue covering most of the interior was fish excretion. R.J. had "borrowed" the van from someone in the business of buying and selling fresh fish. Although I'd smelled the pungent odor before, it still made me want to retch.

Pushing me flat against the filthy slats, R.J. began methodically cross-lacing a length of rope through a half-dozen eye-loops bolted into the vehicle's floor and side-walls. With every loop, he made several winds around another part of my body, pinning me against the floor.

"That's too tight," I whined. "I can barely breathe."

"That's my girl. Got to keep you from hurting yourself." He jerked on the rope, pulling it tighter.

"You're the one doing all the hurting. And you seem to have a real knack for it." I tried to shift, to relieve the pinch from the nylon cord cutting into my thighs.

"Stop moving!" He slapped my leg with his open hand—hard. "You know how this works. You need to cooperate. Right now, the captain doesn't consider you a runner. He thinks the waves took you out of the raft."

He pulled a separate piece of rope through his fingers and formed a make-shift noose. In seconds, it was snug around my neck. "I'll leave it loose unless you give me trouble. But if you try to fuck with me . . ." He yanked it tight, the compression cutting deep into my windpipe.

Pain shot through my neck, the agony of wrenched vertebra setting fire to my spine. Unable to scream, I thrashed against the restraints.

Okay, that's enough! I get it.

But it wasn't enough, not for R.J.

Powerless to speak, I pleaded with my eyes, waiting for him to release the pressure.

Wrapping the loose end of the rope around his knuckles, he leaned back, increasing the tension, a smile spreading across his face.

Overwhelmed by a frantic need for air, my pulse hammering in my head, I opened and closed my lips, desperate to tell him I was at the limit of what I could endure.

But his expression revealed the kind of pleasure that can only come at the expense of another's pain. He was not trying to teach me a lesson—*he was enjoying himself.*

Stop! Please stop. I'll do anything you want. I could only think the words, hoping he would get the message.

His mouth widened until he was grinning ear to ear. It was as frightening as the agony of the rope—he might actually be able to read my mind, and was delighted to see me pleading for my life.

The tattletale twitching that precedes seizures from oxygen deprivation began to sweep my body.

The ache of an exploding chest faded to a dull burn, the edges of my vision graying, turning dark. I was back in the sea, on the brink of losing consciousness.

R.J. knew better than to risk brain damage. His sadistic urge to hurt me could reduce my value.

It took several seconds before I realized the tension of the rope was gone. Even so, my bruised and swollen throat made the flow of air raw and painful.

As I lie there, choking back the tears, I swore I would find a way to get through this. I had every right to feel sorry for myself, to cry over the agony of captivity and the pain of outright brutality. But I would not give this sorry excuse for a man the satisfaction of hearing me whimper.

Seemingly pleased with the amount of pain he'd delivered, R.J. threw the end of the choke-rope forward, toward the driver's seat. "Time to hit the trail," he announced.

As we turned onto the main road, I imagined the van emerging from the row of trees lining the Morrison driveway, and behind us, off to the side of the house, Maria's garden, where I'd watched her water the anthuriums the last three mornings.

Part of me wanted to return—to set things right between Morrison and myself. But the thought of leaving Maria a widow, hurting her the way her husband had hurt me.

I couldn't think about it. Not now.

The rough road pounded my face with constant vibration as R.J. steered the van toward every pothole and rut he saw, knowing the impact translated directly to my skull.

Unable to turn away from the foul stench permeating the floorboards, I kept fighting the nausea, the thought of lying in my own vomit a powerful incentive to controlling my stomach.

"Won't be much longer now." R.J.'s voice carried the uplifting encouragement of a parent talking to a backseat full of kids on the way to a Saturday afternoon picnic.

"Where are you taking me?" I croaked, my voice hard to recognize.

He ignored me, absorbed in the country western CD playing in the background.

My neck stung from rope burn, and every swallow was agonizing. Yet I knew my injuries were only a sample of what he was capable of. But I hated R.J. more than I feared him. Not only for what he'd done to me, but for making me cower under the constant threat of more punishment—for intimidating me with the promise of more pain.

I refused to live with that.

Hoping it would irritate the hell out of him, I began to sing along, softly at first—it was the best I could do with a raw throat—and out of key, intentionally mixing up the words, whether I knew them or not.

R.J. turned up the volume. But I continued my screeching, and even though I was unable to compete with the increased sound level, my voice was still there, annoying him.

He switched the music off. I realized he was waiting for me to stop, as if my sarcastic caterwauling would also respond to the controls on the dash.

"Are you forgetting about the rope around your neck?" He tugged on it, making me wince. While I knew he wouldn't hesitate to add new bruises, I also knew the captain would examine each one, wanting an explanation for the severity, the reasons for damaging the merchandise. Once again, I was an asset, and keeping me in good condition was paramount to bringing the highest possible price.

"I want to know how much longer you're going to keep me tied up," I said. "These cuffs are killing me."

"Shoulda thought of that before mouthing off to Morrison. Especially about his son. You had no reason to do that."

"No reason? He set me up so you could kidnap me and take me to God knows where. He's a piece of shit."

"He fished you out of the ocean. Saved your life. You forget about that?"

"Yeah, I owe him plenty. And some day, I'll repay him for his kindness."

"So tell me the truth . . . you really fuck his kid?"

"What difference does it make?"

"I saw the kid at the dock. He had a fuzzy, dumb look on his face. On somebody that young, it usually means he's just been laid. Thought maybe you'd done him a favor. You know, let him fuck a real woman."

His comment struck me as a blatant contradiction. "You don't have the right to call me a *real woman*. To you, I'm a piece of meat, something you can sell by the pound." My last few words barely made it out. My throat was going to need some time to heal.

"Hey, bitch, this is business. And in this part of the world, it's the only kind of business that pays. You think I'm gonna waste my time driving a taxi or washing dishes in some shit-hole bar? I do this to stay alive. Listen to me, you prissy little cunt, if you get hungry enough, you'll do whatever it takes to put food in your mouth. So don't give me any more of your holier-than-thou attitude."

I refused to answer him. But he was right.

On the *Kelsey*, I'd done whatever was necessary to survive. I hadn't forgotten the choices I'd made. But I'd put those experiences behind me.

After spending three days with Maria, I no longer thought of myself as a runaway slave. As far as I was concerned, I'd regained the right to choose my own future. The reality of being returned to captivity, at the mercy of another's whims, hadn't sunk in. It was the reason I was ready to fight. Even bound and tied to the floor, I wanted to strike back. More than that, I wanted to punish every man who had helped put me in the back of this truck.

But I knew the truth. My need to hurt R.J.—to claw at him, to set my nails into his eye sockets—would not serve me. At least not now. If I was going to reclaim the leverage I'd earned on the *Kelsey*, I had to resume the guise of a broken spirit, ready to obey. In short, I had to change my approach. And I had to start immediately.

I tried to neutralize my voice, not to mask the raspy hoarseness, but to conceal the streak of defiance bubbling just under the surface. "So, the captain sent you to find me, huh?"

The question surprised R.J. and he took a moment before answering. "He put out a reward."

"How much?"

"A thousand bucks. Enough to wake up the street trash so they'd keep their eyes open."

"I thought you told him I'd drowned. If the captain believed you, why the reward?"

"Standard practice when there's no body. If a girl disappears, the owner offers a reward. Clears things up."

Now I understood. The captain's intention of posting a reward was not to insure my safe return, but to confirm my death. He never expected to find me alive. His offer of a thousand dollars—even for my corpse—was his way of arriving at a warped sense of economic closure.

"So you were able to pick up the captain before the *Kelsey* went down?" I asked.

"Not me. The cargo ship dropped life rafts all over the area. The captain managed to find one. When I heard you'd made it to shore, I figured you'd done the same thing. But Morrison said something about finding you floating on some wreckage."

"Yeah, I was lucky." My voice was laced with sarcasm. I reminded myself to pull back, play the part. "What about Annie? Did she make it to a raft?" The renewed possibility of

Annie's survival came from simple logic—if the captain had found a raft, maybe Annie did, too.

R.J. was quiet for a few seconds. "The captain put out the same reward for her. If she made it to the coast, someone will find her and turn her in. But it's been three days. Not much chance now."

He talked about her as if she were a lost dog—unsure if she were alive. The promise of a thousand dollars would answer the question and decide the outcome. If no one claimed the reward, the captain would cross Annie off his list and close the books on her account.

"You knew her for over two years," I said. "Don't you feel anything for her? Won't you miss her?"

"Yeah, I'll miss her tight butt sliding between the tables, serving us dinner every night."

Bastard.

To him, Annie had been nothing more than a quick piece of ass, some *thing* he'd used to get his rocks off. I'd forgotten how cruel and calculating these men could be. Money was their only motivator. Emotions like pity and sympathy had no place in their business plan.

I had to put my thoughts of Annie away. She would always be with me, but I couldn't allow her memory to mix with the same anger and revulsion I felt for the men who had shanghaied us. Right now, I needed that hate to spread through me like a miracle drug, keeping me strong—and ready.

The van began to slow. It seemed too soon to be *anywhere*, but even a rest stop would be welcome, as long as I could stretch my legs. The ropes were killing me, and I needed to get off the floor.

"Are we near Yangon already?" I knew it was unlikely, but R.J. hadn't revealed our destination, and I hoped my question would prompt him to give me some idea of where we were headed.

"Nope."

"So why are we stopping?"

"I need to check on something."

"What is it? The engine overheating?" A breakdown could work to my advantage.

"Yeah, it's the engine." His words were dripping with deception. He was placating me. There was nothing wrong with the van. He was up to something.

"What's going on, R.J.?"

I heard a bouncy squeak as he unlatched the glove compartment door. He began rummaging through loose keys, spare change, and other collected junk.

"What are you looking for?"

The answer came in the form of a *snap*, probably from a tightly sealed plastic lid. Whatever he was searching for, he'd found it.

The driver's door opened.

"Where are you going?"

"Got something for you."

What the hell does that mean? Is this a midday fuck Jewel break? Or was he going to sit on me again so he could cinch the ropes even tighter, completely shutting off the circulation to my arms and legs?

The rear doors flew open. R.J. was holding something, but it was outside my line of sight.

"Shoulda done this a lot sooner. Wasn't sure there was enough left to do any good, but there's a nice, full dose." He brought the syringe up to my face, letting me see.

My throat was closing, my chest refusing to draw air. "Why, R.J.? Why are you doing this to me?"

His voice turned raw. "I'm doing you a favor, bitch, letting you sleep for the rest of the trip. Wish I could say the same for myself."

I felt the sting of the needle pierce my hip. "Ouch!"

"Hmmm, must've hit a nerve. I'll try a different spot."

He was playing, spearing me with an 18 gauge needle.

"Stop it, dammit! You're hurting me."

"Quit squirming." He grabbed my ass with his free hand and jabbed me again. "How's that feel?"

"It hurts like hell, you fucking asshole!"

He twisted the syringe, pushing it deeper until the skin depression reached the muscle. "You've got a bad case of smart mouth, but I've got the cure for that."

Chapter Eight

"Drop the clothes."

I removed them without hesitation.

The captain circled his finger in the air, indicating he wanted me to turn so he could inspect every inch of me.

I'd cringed as he'd walked into the room. He'd seen it. I didn't care.

I'd thought—hoped—he was dead, in an optimistic, *the-world-would-be-better-off-because-of-it* kind of way. Finding him alive was like standing face-to-face with an ancient evil that refused to die, no matter how many stakes pierced his heart.

"Where are we?"

"Lampang."

"You're kidding, right? That's in Thailand."

The captain didn't flinch.

"How long was I out?" I rubbed the black and blue marks on my hip.

"Doesn't matter. You're here now, and that's what counts."

R.J. had driven me across the border of Burma and into the very center of Thailand, a distance of six-hundred-fifty miles. Lashed to the van's floorboards for over thirteen hours, I'd absorbed every jarring bump and jolt from the poorly-maintained roads.

The captain turned his head and did a double take on my butt. "You picked up a few bruises and scrapes, but nothing serious. You'll be ready by next week."

What about the ugly blue streaks around my neck? I wanted to tell him how R.J. had put them there. I even thought of embellishing the story, accusing him of slamming me against the floorboards for the sheer pleasure of it, then back-handing me so he could enjoy the feel of his knuckles smashing into my face.

I doubted it would make a difference. The captain knew what a thousand dollars would buy, not only in terms of getting his property returned, but also in regard to how the goods would be treated. The fact there was no permanent damage was all that mattered.

"We're staying here three nights," the captain said, his distracted manner making it seem as if he were talking to himself. "You'll have the room to yourself."

Here was a run-down hotel in the older district of Lampang. Years ago, the building was probably a cheap boarding house, hosting young travelers and a few intrepid tourists on a budget. Some of them had come to visit the temples and other historic sites, while others—mostly men—were surely lured by stories of easy-to-score hashish and transgendered women, their need to experience the intoxication of a smoking parlor or the thrill of having sex with a lady-boy often leaving them disappointed—or worse.

Now, the dilapidated building served as a sex-trafficking halfway house. Designated an unofficial neutral zone, the rooms were used by slave traders to get their girls rested and ready for passage to the next port. It was a place where deals were struck, where the law never entered, and where untrained girls were housed while they completed their "education."

My room was small and dingy. The original color of the walls—some variation of off-white—was hidden under a gray mask of accumulated cigarette smoke and burned residue from free-based cocaine. The single bed sagged noticeably in the middle, and the only window was glazed with a piece of wire-mesh security glass.

The place smelled like death.

"From here, we'll drive south to the coast. The Thailand broker will have my new boat ready the end of the week," the captain continued. "I need to be there to take possession, sign the papers."

"What happens then?" I wanted him to know I was paying attention.

"There's an auction, on Saturday."

My throat clenched, the air seizing in my chest. I dug my nails into my palm, hoping I could hide it. "Another auction? So soon? I look like hell."

"Can't be helped. That's the schedule."

He didn't care that my bruises would still be visible. He was determined to sell me as soon as possible. He needed the money to pay for insurance deductibles, provisioning, and other under-the-table fees to insure the boat's paperwork would be filed quickly and without a lot of scrutiny.

"What about your crew? Did they make it through the storm?" Truthfully, I didn't care. I suppose I should have, as one human being cares about another. But I didn't. The only reason I asked was to work my way toward what I really wanted to know—*what happened to Annie?*

"We lost quite a few. Dumb bastards tried to cut their way through the sails, work underneath the sheets to get to the forward raft. Current got 'em."

"But some survived, right?"

The captain glared at me. Perhaps he considered the information privileged, beyond my need to know. Finally, he said, "The *Kochi Mar* dropped rafts around the area. So far, three men have been picked up."

I couldn't wait any longer. "And Annie?"

He paused, much longer than it should take to search such a short-lived memory. "Nothing yet."

I felt my stomach sink. It was all he was going to say. I decided to leave it alone—for now.

Not caring that he was watching, I walked to the door and jiggled the handle, testing the lock, then realized how silly it was to think that a flimsy, worn-out piece of hardware would stop anyone from coming in. I looked back at the broken bed and, for a moment, wondered how circumstances, or fate, or my own stupidity had brought me to this horrible little room. I could only hope this was the first step to finding my way home. Maybe in a month or two, I would look back on the memory of this shit-hole with a kind of reverent gratitude. But for now, it was my prison, and escape didn't seem likely.

"So when you said I'm supposed to stay here for the next three nights, are you talking about right here, in this room?"

The captain looked at me the way a stern schoolmaster stares at a natural troublemaker—there would be no second chances. "Make sure you're in this bed every night by ten. The only way in or out of the building is through the lobby, and I'll have two men down there at all times."

"You're giving me free run of the place?"

The captain's expression hardened. "Jewel, you need to understand something, and it's for your own good. Even if you were able to make it outside the building, there's not much chance you'd survive. A young girl on the street in this part of town doesn't last long. We'd eventually find you, but the kind of shape you'd be in, or if you were still alive . . . well, that's the question, isn't it?"

I looked at him with exaggerated confusion. "It couldn't be that bad."

The captain was growing impatient. "Alright, no more sugarcoating it. The reward I offered, I've got no way to retract it. And if the street rats catch you, they'll eventually turn you in, but not until they've used you in ways you can't imagine. Inside this building, I can protect you."

Now I understood. As far as the slaver's informal network of thugs was concerned, I was a runaway. If I managed to make it outside the hotel, they would be waiting, ready to grab me on sight.

"What about food?"

"You hungry?"

I really wasn't, but I was toying with the idea of getting a message to a waiter or even a guy delivering take-out. "I will be, later."

"One of the men will bring something in. You'll eat with the rest of us." He started for the door, finished.

"Okay if I take a look around?"

"Suit yourself. Remember, in bed by ten. If you disobey me, I'll lock you in this room until we're ready to leave."

With that, he disappeared into the hall.

Chapter Nine

The *lobby,* as the captain had called it, was no bigger than a typical living room. But that's where the similarity ended. Secure from inside and out, the windows were permanently shuttered and barred. The front entrance reflected the same degree of fortification, with thick steel strapping reinforcing the door and jamb.

Overhead, dingy fluorescent fixtures hung from the ceiling, their winking bulbs creating an epileptic nightmare. Holes in the drywall gave testimony to scuffles and altercations settled on the spot, the occasional red stain on the gritty concrete floor a reminder that not all arguments had ended amicably.

A closet-sized room—more of a cage, really—stood in the corner near the front door. Measuring about five-by-six feet, the walls were a framework of unpainted two-by-fours covered with heavy wire mesh. A small cut-out provided a portal for an exchange of money and keys.

Usually occupied by a heavy-set balding man with a pock-marked face and permanently soured expression, his surly manner and gruff appearance was more than enough to discourage those not in need of the hotel's unusual features. But in case the lost and misguided refused to heed the obvious clues provided by the venomous atmosphere and the street-tough patrons, a small faded sign confirmed the absence of a pubic bathroom or phone.

The lodging policy was simple: Cash only, no refunds, and complaints were ignored.

To the right of the cage, an old vending machine stood empty and unplugged, its broken glass panel covered with a large "Out of Order" sticker. It was obvious the adhesive-backed label served more to hold the shards of loose glass in place than to prevent someone from trying to use the derelict machine.

The only furniture in the room was a ratty couch pushed into the far corner, away from the entrance. Never used, the men who constantly occupied the room stayed on their feet. Methodically pacing or leaning against the walls, their trance-like demeanor was interrupted only by the single handed replacement of a cigarette burning short enough to warm their fingers. Obviously in charge of security, they made on-the-spot decisions about who could enter or leave the building.

I noticed while the identities of the men might change, the room seemed regulated by strict rules of occupancy. Four men—no more, no less—standing, smoking, watching. Two of the men worked for the captain, but I didn't know which ones. And I wasn't going to ask.

My roaming privileges weren't such an advantage after all. The captain had bound me with a virtual rope of fear and intimidation, and it was every bit as effective as the chain he'd used to stretch me out in the *Kelsey*'s hold.

For now, I would stay out of the lobby.

Chapter Ten

I hadn't slept much, only a couple of hours. The walls between the rooms were thin and the conversations loud. Sometimes the voices were exclusively male. Other times, the breaking voice of a young girl was unmistakable. On the floor below me, the activity was constant, with footfalls and slamming doors frequently co-mingled with the sucking draw of a toilet.

But it wasn't only the noise that kept me up. As I laid there on that foul, tattered mattress, my mind had raced back to years before, to another tearful and sleepless night. Although the circumstances were different, the hurt was the same. Back then, I'd been cut to the quick by a thoughtless question about the sudden death of my parents—someone wanting to know if the impact from the collision had killed them instantly or if they were alive—still aware—when the fire swept through the car.

The question had come on the morning of their funeral, making the situation even more unbearable. I'd barely held myself together through the service and reception that followed, reminding myself to thank friends and neighbors for their condolences, pretending to admire the flowers, and enduring the predictable words of encouragement offered by departing guests.

At the time, I couldn't have felt more alone. But I got through it. And as the months passed, I found the comfort that came from a lingering hug or a heartfelt note from a friend. Eventually, those who truly cared about me restored my faith in the world, reminding me that life was still worth living.

But here, I had no one. And as I reached out with both hands, I found only the edges of a thread-worn mattress on a single bed There was no space for compassion, no room for hugs, no place for someone to sit next to me and give me hope.

Looking out into the darkness through tear-filled eyes, it was easy to imagine Annie's ghostly image at the end of the bed, her spirit unable to speak, her outreached hand unable to touch. I would have given anything to hear her voice, to take strength in her promise—*No matter what, we'll get through this . . . together.*

Chapter Eleven

My second day came and went without any personal contact between myself and the captain. And while the crew's presence was obvious—walking the halls, checking my room, watching me as I retrieved a bottle of water—I was relieved to find their motivation strictly business. No unnecessary conversation or interaction. It was the same with everyone in the hotel, with one exception—a middle-aged man who, by either circumstance or plan, followed me into the dormitory-style bathroom.

The shared unisex facility provided stall showers and narrow alcoves with toilets, but not a lot of privacy. Wary that he might expect me to service him, I confronted him at the door, letting him know I would appreciate if he would wait outside until I was finished.

"No! I'm not waiting," he blustered, his voice colored with a British matter-of-fact urgency. "I have smattering little interest in what you're up to. I just need to take a shit." With that, he pushed past me, rushed into the nearest open stall and squatted on the toilet.

Seeing the matter was non-negotiable, I walked to the opposite end of the room and pretended to straighten my makeup, waiting for him to finish.

"You being traded?" His attempt at casual conversation surprised me.

I nodded into the mirror.

"You're a damn fine looking girl. You'll bring a good price."

It was a compliment, but I said nothing. Acknowledging his attempt to flatter me while he moved his bowels was beyond my comprehension. Perhaps someday I would learn to appreciate his raw admiration, after the repeated scenes of buying and selling girls had made me numb to the slightest trace of human dignity, and when my own conversation had deteriorated into talking about the number of tricks I'd done.

It was a day I hoped would never come.

It was around midnight—right after a particularly noisy exchange between the downstairs proprietor and a new customer who didn't want to pay the full rate for a second room—when I realized the unusual opportunity the captain had given me. During the hours dedicated to sleeping, I was unsupervised. I knew better than to try to dig my way out with a spoon. But behind my closed door, I had seven uninterrupted hours to think and plan.

I began with what I already knew, to determine if there was something I'd overlooked, something I could use to plot an escape.

I realized I'd underestimated the power of money in a country where poverty was the norm. The promise of quick cash was a potent motivator. Payoffs and reward money fueled a street-network that was always watching, always waiting for the opportunity to make a quick hundred for a simple phone call. It was unsophisticated and relied on technology no more complex than a cell phone. But its eyes were everywhere. The slave trade was such an accepted part of life, that everyone— shopkeepers, residents, even school kids—saw it as an opportunity to score hard cash for reporting anything unusual. I even overheard one of the men in the hotel refer to it as the country's version of the lottery, where anyone could play, and you didn't need to buy a ticket to win.

Now I understood why Annie had initially discouraged me from running. And after my experience with Morrison, I had learned the hardest lesson of all—I couldn't trust anyone.

About two in the morning, I started thinking about the men who constantly occupied the downstairs lobby. Although it went against my protective instincts, I realized one of those silent behemoths might be a potential confederate. I knew better than to outright ask for their cooperation. But if I could talk one of them into passing along a note or mailing a letter for me, it would be my version of a message in a bottle, detailing my predicament and revealing my location.

While I didn't have any money to pay an amenable goon for his "act of kindness," there was another kind of currency I could offer. More than once Annie had reminded me how the majority of men were easily persuaded with the promise of a woman's body. The thought wasn't pretty, but neither was the picture of my future. If that was the price I had to pay to get my life back, the sooner the better.

I'd found the stubby remains of a pencil under the dresser. Putting my hands on a piece of paper could be a problem. I'd noticed a notepad inside the lobby cage, but stealing a sheet wouldn't be easy—the wire booth was locked when unoccupied, and the resident gorilla had shooed me away the few times I'd offered a "good morning" or "hello." Maybe if I dropped a wad of gum on the floor, then asked for something to clean it up . . .

It was a long shot, but it was all I could think of.

Writing the note would be easy. Deciding who should receive it would not. After an hour of racking my brain, my frustration finally gave way to an unlikely but logical choice—my old high school civics teacher. He would remember me and surely feel an obligation to pass the note along to the authorities. It could take weeks before it ended up in the right hands, but it would be a start.

Chapter Twelve

"I want you dressed and ready in ten minutes. You understand?"

I'd been asleep less than two hours. Groggy and fighting against the sudden intrusion, I struggled to make sense of who was talking and what they wanted.

My eyes finally focused on the captain. He was standing inside the door. His appearance in the room—without so much as a single knock on the door—confirmed his complete lack of respect for my privacy.

"What'd'ya want?" I wailed. "It's still dark outside." I pulled the covers up tight around my shoulders, reluctant to give up the small amount of security provided by the rag-worn sheet and ripped bedspread.

"Change of plans. We're leaving. Get up, now!"

"Why so early?"

"It's a seven hour trip and I want to be there by noon."

"Seven hours? Where are we going?"

He hesitated. "Bangkok."

"I thought we were staying here another day, until your new boat was ready. What's the rush?" The thought of dragging myself out of bed before sunrise was no more appealing than the day-old reheated pot-stickers I'd had last night for dinner.

"I don't have time for questions. Get your ass out of bed and put these on." He tossed a wadded ball of fabric and baseball cap on the mattress.

"Jesus, what kind of bug crawled up your ass?"

"You're wasting time," he growled. "I said ten minutes."

Apparently, he was going to wait. I flipped back the covers and slid out of bed.

"Doesn't sound like there's going to be time for breakfast," I mumbled.

"You can eat when we get there. Now put on the clothes."

I shook out the twisted roll of cloth and held it out in front of me—a faded brown sack-dress. The thing looked like a prison uniform. I grimaced, forming a mental picture of it hanging off my shoulders. "Latest from Neiman-Marcus? It's at least three sizes too big."

"It'll keep you covered. Less obvious."

I knew the real reason for his choice of fashion as well as he did. The generic clothing would make it less likely someone would remember me leaving the building, especially if the police were eventually persuaded to trace my whereabouts.

"I have to pee. You going with me to the john, or you gonna let me do that by myself?"

The captain scowled. "Hurry up. But if you're gone longer than three minutes, I'm dragging you out of there."

I wrapped the dress around me like a towel. Under the circumstances, demonstrating any form of modesty was silly at best. But I wanted to make it clear that even though I'd lost my liberty, I'd retained my independence. I was cooperating in spite of the captain's belligerent attitude, and I wanted him to realize it.

"Three minutes," he repeated.

I resisted the urge to slam the door behind me. It would only serve to irritate him, and for some reason, he was already in a bad mood.

I used the toilet and hurriedly washed my face. Glancing in the dirty mirror, it occurred to me the captain might try to neutralize my appearance by shearing my hair to a boyish length. I piled it on top of my head, securing it with an elastic head-band.

I was surprised to find him waiting in my room. As I came through the door, he frowned, looking at his watch. Whatever was pushing him out of the hotel was making him nervous as hell.

I pulled the black ball-cap down tight around my temples. "What's with the early checkout? Your new boat ready?"

"Too many people know you're here. I'm sure some of the locals overhead the crew talking about our schedule. We're getting out now. Safer that way."

His tone was ominous, as if he expected a gang of thugs to be waiting for us outside the building. "Should I be worried? Are you sure this is a good idea?"

The captain threw me a warning glance. I was questioning his judgment, and he didn't like it.

"The crew's downstairs," he barked. "Let's go."

I took a quick look around the room. I'd checked out of many hotel rooms, but this time, there was no reason to look in the closets for forgotten shirts or in the dresser for an overlooked tube of lipstick. I had nothing but the clothes on my back. And even those didn't belong to me.

"What are you looking for?" The captain's voice reeked with impatience.

"Nothing," I mumbled. "Nothing I'll ever miss."

Downstairs, R.J. and two new crewmembers I didn't recognize were waiting. Neither of the new men looked like sailors. The first lacked the hard-won credentials of sun-damaged skin and calloused hands. Middle-aged and balding, he could have been a high school English teacher undergoing a mid-life crisis. Shifting from one foot to the other, he appeared anxious, impatient to show off a passion for his new line of work.

"What's your name?" I asked.

The sudden twitch of his forehead told me he wasn't expecting conversation. At least not from me.

"Wendell," he stammered.

"Hello, Wendell." *Who the fuck names their kid Wendell?*

The other crewman was young, mid-twenties. Of obvious Spanish heritage, he was dark with fine, distinct features and black, wavy hair. I couldn't ignore the irony that under the circumstances, he struck me as handsome. Watching me with shy concern, he seemed uncomfortable, inexperienced.

I offered a whispered, "Hi."

He tipped his head, letting me know he heard.

"My name is Jewel," I added. "What's yours?" I produced a smile.

"I'm Tomas," he answered. "It's ahhh . . . nice to meet you."

I could tell he regretted it the moment he said it. There was nothing nice about any of this. I was a sex slave, a piece of merchandise—and it was nice to meet me? He glanced at the other men, then looked down at the floor, their silent mocking of his gullible innocence leaving him embarrassed.

"Where's the van?" The captain broke the awkward silence.

"At the end of the block," R.J. answered.

The captain shook his head. "That's at least two hundred yards."

"It's as close as I could get," R.J. added. "Marco's waiting behind the wheel."

"The street clear?"

"Nobody in sight."

"You're sure? You checked both sides?"

They were talking about a distance of 600 feet. And yet, the captain was concerned, even worried about getting from the hotel to the van in one piece.

"Street's empty," R.J. answered. "Want Marco to do a drive by and pick us up out front?"

The captain paused, thinking. "No. If there's someone watching, they'll ID the plate."

He didn't just suspect trouble, he was anticipating it. The crew's slip of the tongue—revealing our departure schedule—had been a major security breach. The irony had to be biting him in the ass—if there *was* someone out there waiting to grab me, they would be the very same people to whom he'd promised a reward for my return. Now he had to hide me from the network of eyes he usually depended on to find runaway slaves.

"Take her out." For a moment, I didn't realize the captain was talking about me. It was the same thing he would say when ordering his first mate to lift anchor and set sail.

Even in the dull, gray light, I saw the glint of polished steel as Wendell pulled a pair of handcuffs from his pocket.

I offered up both hands in a show of cooperation. "I won't give you any trouble."

Wendell compressed the first bracelet around my wrist, the rapid clicking of the ratchet followed by enough pressure to make me flinch.

He pushed my other hand away. "You're chained to me," he said, securing the remaining cuff to his left wrist.

"We'll need this for insurance, to keep her quiet." R.J. held up a ball-gag and head-strap.

I felt the same crippling terror that left me faint and nauseous that first morning on the *Kelsey*. It was a reminder of how these men could do anything they wanted, without fear of reprisal or accountability. Worse, R.J. had hurt me before, leaving his mark on both my memory and my throat. From the hopeful expectation in his voice, I knew nothing would give him greater pleasure than to do it again.

I turned to the captain. "You don't need the gag. I won't make a sound, I promise."

"Do it," Wendell said. "Gag her." His eyes were wide and anxious. He was panting like a dog. The prospect of seeing me bound and gagged had excited him to the point of arousal. "Once we get her outside," he continued, "we don't want the bitch screaming her lungs out."

He was revealing himself to be a sadistic bastard. I hoped it would make him careless and distracted—a definite advantage if an opportunity presented itself.

R.J. stepped behind me, bringing the two-inch rubber ball to my chin. "Wendell's right. She could start screaming the minute we're outside."

My stomach was turning, my legs threatening to buckle. "Captain, I swear you won't hear a peep out of me."

The captain was hesitating. He knew I would fight R.J.'s efforts to gag me. He was probably deliberating over the effect a few more bruises could have on my final value at auction.

"Please," I begged. "I'll do exactly as you say." I raised my free hand and brought a single finger to my lips, feigning a whisper. "Not a word," I added.

R.J. pushed my hand away from my face. "Fuck this bullshit. Wendell, grab her head."

"NO!" I shrieked, clamping my mouth shut.

Forcing the ball-gag against my lips, R.J. snarled. "Come on, you little shit, open up."

My words came through bared teeth, stifled, and lacking their normal sharp vindictive edge, but the meaning was clear. "Fuck off."

Wendell tightened his grip, holding my head steady against the increasing pressure of the hard rubber. "You crazy bitch. You're just making it worse."

The corners of R.J.'s mouth turned upward in a devilish grin. "I was going to leave it loose, but now . . ." His fingers raked at my jaw, determined to force it open.

Needle-sharp pain shot through my lower lip, a dribble of warm fluid trickling down my chin, the tattle-tale taste of metallic copper confirming my mouth was full of blood.

"That's enough," the captain ordered. "She could lose a tooth. That'll mean less money."

He'd weighed the cost of insuring my silence against a possible loss of value at auction. He'd decided to take the risk.

Maybe the blood had helped.

R.J. was more than disappointed. Not ready to quit, he kept up the pressure, holding the gag tight against my swollen, bleeding mouth. "Get this straight, sweet thing. Once we're on the street, I don't want to hear a single word out of you."

R.J.'s stale, rancid breath fell heavy on my face. I shut my eyes, trying to block it out.

"You listening to me, bitch?" His fingers clawed at my eyelids, forcing them open. "Not a word, understand? Otherwise, you and me are gonna have us a party." He shook the ball-gag in front of my face.

Asshole. I almost said it.

It wasn't all I wanted to say. I wanted to tell him about my *list*, and how he was quickly rising to the top—a dubious honor since he would be the first to receive retribution for what he'd done to me.

My mouth was contorted in a bloody snarl. I did my best to relax my expression, hoping to manage a blank stare. I wanted to validate the captain's decision. He was the only person who could keep this sadistic lunatic under control.

The captain's complacent acceptance of R.J.'s behavior surprised me. While restraint and implied threats of punishment had been an integral part of the training program, I had rarely experienced outright physical violence while in the captain's presence. But now, with R.J. taking over as disciplinarian, brute force had become the preferred method of assuring my obedience. R.J.'s increased authority was also confusing. There had been others on the ship with more experience and seniority— unless they'd been lost in the storm. There was only one other reason I could think of: It had been his reward for returning me.

Chapter Thirteen

The move from the hotel to the van was executed like a precision military maneuver. With R.J. advancing to point, Tomas secured the area behind. Wendell and the captain kept me between them, shuffling me forward twenty feet at a time, and only after a signal from R.J. indicating the cars ahead were empty, the alleyways vacant, and the storefronts unoccupied.

At first, I assumed the shadows might be hiding a street pimp on a recruiting mission or an opportunist watching for runaways. But their real worry was a confrontation with Lampang's violent underworld—armed strike teams who would think nothing of relieving the captain of his cargo.

I did exactly as I was told. I even pretended to watch for activity on the street, occasionally offering a whispered assessment of unoccupied windows and empty rooftops. I wanted to substantiate the captain's trust. I had given him my promise of cooperation, and by making good on it, I would more likely earn his protection. Without it, I could easily find myself at the mercy of R.J., who was surely waiting for the next opportunity to subject me to his own special brand of discipline.

"Tie her to the floorboards," the captain ordered. Then turning to me, he added, "Until we're out of town. It's safer that way."

Offering a quick nod to indicate I understood, I climbed into the back of the van. Wendell released the handcuffs and followed me in.

"On your stomach," Wendell ordered.

Pressing me against the stinking floor-slats with his knee, he began working the nylon line through the tie-downs as he looped it around my wrists and ankles.

My stomach sank as R.J. joined him.

"Make it tight. Pull out every inch of slack."

I knew R.J. was looking at my neck, wanting to leash my throat with the same noose he used before. Whether he was concerned he would add to the purple bruises he'd previously inflicted or he didn't want to risk his actions being vetoed by the captain, I was relieved when he simply shook the rope in front of my face, making the threat clear and certain.

"All comfy?" Wendell asked.

"I can't move, if that's what you mean."

For a moment, Wendell looked as if he might back-hand me for mouthing off. Instead, he squeezed my face, forcing my lips to pucker. "Very soon, my pretty. Very soon."

He'd been taking his cues from R.J., and was anxious to demonstrate what he'd learned.

Wendell sat in the front passenger seat next to Marco. As I'd climbed into the van, I'd glimpsed Marco's full head of wavy, bottle-bleached hair. From the generous amount of space between him and the headliner, he couldn't be much over five-foot-eight.

"Where you want me to sit?" Tomas had been waiting off to the side, watching the street while Wendell and R.J. bound me to the floor. With the left rear seat occupied by R.J.—so he could keep an eye on me, he'd said—and the captain taking the remaining empty rear seat, Tomas was the odd man out.

"Climb in next to Jewel," the captain said. "You can keep her company."

Tomas chose his footing carefully, trying not to step on me. He settled close, his legs spreading over mine as he leaned back against the side-wall. I felt his hand slide over my back.

I couldn't tell if he was reassuring me or testing me to see if I would object.

"Don't go over the speed limit," the captain warned Marco. "Some of the cops work the trade. And the ones who don't will want to know why we have a white girl tied up in the back."

We'd just pulled away from the curb, and already the captain's concern had shifted away from having to deal with street gangs to the risk of being discovered with a bound captive in the back of his vehicle.

It should have made a difference to me, but it didn't. If there had been an element of danger in this early morning ride out of Lampang, I hadn't seen it. I even thought about telling them how silly they'd looked on the street, like a bunch of little boys pretending to be on a spy mission. But my mouth was throbbing from R.J.'s brutal assault, and my right arm ached from the compression of the rope. I also knew R.J. was waiting for any excuse to resume his attack on me, relishing the opportunity to demonstrate his new authority—not to mention the sadistic pleasure he would receive from watching me bleed.

For now, I would remain quiet.

For the last two days, I'd experienced a limited sense of freedom. Although unable to leave the hotel, I'd been free to walk the halls, take bathroom breaks, and visit the inhospitable lobby. When I was hungry, I could pick up a piece of stale, leftover pizza from the small refrigerator located inside a dingy storeroom. But now, I was truly a captive—again. Separated from the other occupants in the vehicle by rope and pain, these men did not consider me their equal. Hell, as far as they were concerned, I wasn't even human—because humans weren't treated this way.

No, I was wrong.

There *were* treated this way. And it was something I would never forget.

As I lie there, lashed to the same rancid floorboard I'd been forced to endure on the trip from Morrison's home to the hotel, I said my last goodbyes, allowing my subconscious to finally burn the bridge between who I was and who I'd been forced to become. I did it out of necessity, shutting down feelings, blurring memories, lessening the pull of my past.

This wasn't the first time I'd "adjusted" my character and temperament. The process had started the moment I'd regained consciousness on the *Kelsey* and found myself hog-tied in the bottom of a drainage pit. I knew I had to insulate myself from the psychological trauma of being kidnapped. I had to find a way to manage the fear and the numbing disbelief that this was really happening—to me. But even as I'd reinforced my resistance and stamina, I'd reassured myself the situation was temporary, and my newly contrived attitude and behavior were merely a smokescreen to hide the real me from being permanently harmed. I would drop the pretense when I returned to my old life.

Now, I couldn't imagine going back. Everything familiar was gone. Even my sense of identity had been taken from me. I was no longer that optimistic twenty-three-year-old girl who'd grown up on the beach in San Diego. For the life of me, I couldn't revive the memories—the enjoyment, the pleasure—of walking along Mission Bay, window shopping in La Jolla, or having lunch at Anthony's while looking out over the harbor.

But there was no point in grieving for the old Jewel. She could not have withstood the mental and physical abuse I'd already endured—and that was no doubt to be a part of my future.

It was a sad consolation, but my transition to someone tougher, stronger, and more resilient had also made me fully capable of retaliating against my enemies. It was a part of me now—the need to extract revenge, to punish those who dared think they could buy and sell a human life. And someday, I would pay the bastards back for what they had done to me.

Chapter Fourteen

"What time is it?" It was Wendell, in the front of the van.

"Seven-thirty," the captain confirmed.

"When are we supposed to be there?" Marco joined the conversation.

"No later than noon," Wendell answered. "Bidding starts at one."

"Shut up!" The captain spoke with the same authority he used to deliver orders from the deck of the *Kelsey*.

"What's the difference?" R.J. asked. "She's gonna find out in a few hours anyway."

It was impossible to misinterpret Wendell's slip of the tongue. *They were taking me to auction!*

I'd hoped to have several more days to prepare, to learn the route of the trip and the physical layout of the auction house—anything that would improve my chances of escape.

I inhaled deeply. I had to stay focused. I might hear something that would make a difference.

I waited until I was sure my voice was steady. "The auction is today?" I said it as nonchalantly as I could, almost in passing, the way I might ask about a clearance sale at Macy's.

The abrupt silence made the breach of secrecy even more obvious. The men had been expected to keep our destination a secret. Wendell's accidental disclosure had set everyone on edge.

I wondered how long the captain had planned to keep it from me—perhaps right up until the last minute, just before throwing me into a cage.

The men shifted nervously in their seats, their movements emphasized by the sudden chorus of popping vinyl.

Finally, the captain turned in his seat. "Are we going to have a problem with this?"

His question surprised me. Rather than an explanation, he'd issued a challenge. If there was any chance of receiving more consideration or his protection during the auction, my answer had to sound truthful. More important, *he* had to believe it.

"You and me," I began, "we had an understanding. We talked about it on the boat. But right now, I'm scared. I had no idea you planned on selling me today. I don't feel ready, and I don't know what to expect. I'm worried about who might buy me, and what kind of life I could have."

I paused, waiting for some kind of response. The captain sat still as stone. Maybe if I asked a question . . .

"I suppose there's the possibility of being bought by someone with a lot of money, like royalty or a rich businessman?"

"Oh, he's rich all right." Wendell again.

"*He's* rich? I don't understand. There's only one buyer?"

"No, Jewel." The captain's voice was unusually soft, as if hoping to keep me from becoming agitated. "There's always dozens of buyers, but there's one in particular who has expressed an interest, and it's based on the pictures I sent him."

Based on the pictures I sent him.

I prayed I was wrong.

After the *Kelsey* was lost at sea, I assumed Gregory had shifted his focus—and his perversions—to another unsuspecting innocent. And besides, *this* auction was in a different country, nearly six hundred miles by car from Yangon, where he'd expected to find me for sale.

I tried to ask without suggesting I knew about the degenerate . . . sadist . . . killer.

"This man you're talking about, is it the same one who asked for the second set of pictures you took of Annie and me?"

"I sent pictures to several buyers. But there's no assurance that any of them will be at the auction. People with that kind of money lead very busy lives. You can't assume any specific buyer is going to show up."

His answer was diplomatic . . . and reeked of deception.

Not good enough.

Surely he'd been in contact with his regular group of buyers and brokers to advise them of when and where he planned to sell me. He should be able to tell me if Gregory was one of them.

"Is there some reason why this particular buyer is more interested than the others?"

"No, Jewel, not really. He's a man with plenty of money, and he tends to outbid the others when he finds a girl he really wants."

The renewed possibility I could wind up in the hands of a killer began to eat away at me, leaving me faint, nauseated. I had to think about something else.

"Anything you can tell me, even a few hints about how the auction works, so I can play it to my advantage?" I held my breath. That didn't sound right—transparent, trying too hard, like over-the-top acting in a high school play.

Wendell started to speak, but the captain cut him off. "There's no hard and fast rules. You'll see the buyers as they enter the building, so you can talk to them if you want to."

"Will any of them ask me questions?"

"A few, but they usually bring their concerns to me. There's not much back-and-forth conversation between the buyers and the girls."

Tomas shifted closer, his hand sliding over my shoulder, giving me a gentle squeeze. His actions were abbreviated—he didn't want the others to see.

I forced a smile. I wasn't sure he could see it, but I wanted to acknowledge his touch.

"Will this be the first time, the first auction, for the other girls, too?" I wanted to keep the captain talking. He might reveal something useful.

Tomas covertly pulled at the ropes across my back to create some slack and make me more comfortable.

The captain didn't answer.

Interpreting his silence as permission to take over, Wendell spoke up, eager to show off his working knowledge of the trade. "Once in a while, you see a *repeater*. It usually means a buyer got bored with the girl and wants something different. So they trade her in on a new model."

Trade her in on a new model. I imagined a late night television commercial where a smartly dressed Asian man with an ear-to-ear smile encouraged the audience to 'come on down and bring their trade-in with them, because this weekend, no reasonable offer would be refused.'

It was sick humor. A way to put my moral and ethical boundaries on hold, shoring up my emotional stability in preparation for what waited for me.

R.J. turned in his seat. "Any more questions, princess?"

His voice was snotty and sarcastic. But I realized the men were waiting for a response. I needed to say something. "Do any of the men ever form emotional attachments to the girls they buy?" It was the best I could do.

"I've never heard of it," Wendell said. "But there's not a lot of customer feedback in this business," he added with a chuckle.

I heard a small laugh from Marco.

The captain said nothing.

I took advantage of the break in the tension. "Any chance you could loosen the ropes? This floor is beginning to get to me. I need to change positions."

Tomas spoke for the first time since entering the van. "What'd'ya think, Captain? Can we trust her?"

The captain drew deep. He didn't like being asked the same question he'd already answered by default. If he'd wanted the ropes removed, he would have said so. I heard the vinyl stretch as he turned slightly in his seat. "Not yet. Let's get a few more miles down the road. I don't want to take the risk of Jewel hurting herself."

I said it without thinking, "Hurt myself? I'd be in a lot less pain without the ropes."

"That's not what I'm talking about." The captain's voice fell slightly, making it clear he was talking only to me. "I mean, if you try to run."

"She's not going to run," Tomas countered. "I'll make sure she stays put."

He'd spoken with bold confidence, and the captain was as surprised as I. His new hire was offering his personal assurance he could do the job, and it had put the captain in an unusual—and difficult—situation. If he denied Tomas the opportunity to prove himself, it would be a summary dismissal, reflecting the captain's lack of confidence in his ability—not to mention embarrassing him in front of the other men.

"She can be a handful," the captain cautioned. "You'll have to watch her like a hawk."

I heard the reluctance in the captain's voice. It was a warning—his implied consent not to be interpreted as weakness.

Tomas leaned toward me, his words intended only for me. "You gonna behave?"

"I promise. I just want off this floor."

He looked back at the captain. "First bit of trouble and I'll cinch her down twice as tight."

The captain took his time. Perhaps he was weighing the pros and cons of giving Tomas a chance to prove himself. More likely, he was evaluating his ability to restrain me if I tried to bolt out the back door. Finally, he spoke. "Go ahead. Untie her."

Tomas looked at me with as much authority as he could muster. "You promised to behave. Remember that." It was for the captain's benefit, not mine.

He began loosening the knots, releasing the tension. In no hurry, his hands drifted over my breasts and hips. I noticed him watching my face, looking for a reaction. I assumed he was testing me, asking my permission, even though we both knew he didn't need it.

I mouthed a silent *thanks.* It wasn't an act. I was truly grateful.

He reached lower, working on the lines securing my legs and ankles. Moving the rope first one way then another, he let one hand linger on my thighs. He reminded me of my first drive-in dates, the boys unsure, yet desperately wanting to caress a firm butt or feel the lips of a wet pussy.

I made the decision on the spot. I would surrender to his advances, give him what he wanted. It was an opportunity to strengthen our unspoken alliance. While I was fairly certain the other men would not scuttle their loyalty to the captain in exchange for sexual favors, I hoped Tomas was different. He was young, his hormones having far more influence on his decisions than the questionable job security offered by the captain.

The resumption of unrestricted blood-flow set my hands and feet tingling. I brought my knees up, reveling in my new freedom, not caring that the sack dress fell back to my waist, exposing the pink bikini underwear from Maria. I wanted him to see them—my way of thanking him for taking a stand against the captain.

His hands swept my legs, his expression serious, focused. I spread my thighs, encouraging him to explore without restriction.

His fingers raced to the damp fabric between my legs, his quick draw of air nearly giving him away. He glanced at the captain, then at R.J. I saw the relief in his face as he confirmed their eyes had remained forward, watching the road.

In some ways, he was every bit a child, excited over the opportunity to play with a new toy. Had we been alone, he would have lost himself in the moment. But with four other men a few feet away—four men who would no doubt want to share in the experience—he remained cautious, careful.

I nodded slightly, confirming my willingness. Until he proved me wrong, I would assume his comparatively gentle, almost tender approach conveyed lustful innocence, his stealth reflecting a desire to bond with me.

I raised my bottom and slid my underwear down, enough to give him access. His fingers raced to my naked vagina. Nervously fiddling with the lips of my pussy, he slid a finger into the inviting wetness.

I watched his face, waiting for him to connect with me. When he finally looked up, his eyes were full of uncertainty, his tense jaw revealing a desperate need for assurance. I smiled, hoping it was enough. I wanted to nourish his young ego, awaken that sense of raw, invincible manhood residing just under the surface of every twenty-something male. Hopefully, it would be the first step in winning his cooperation.

I brought a finger to my pursed lips, confirming our mutual need for secrecy. He agreed with a slight nod of his head, his solemn expression conveying a concern over the lack of privacy. Perhaps he was afraid the captain would disapprove of his advances toward me. I hoped he was trying to conceal the first signs of a willing confederate—a fevered breath away from collusion.

His confidence growing, he slid his fingers in and out of my pussy, finding my clit with his thumb. I feigned an increase in respiration, hoping he would see my rising chest as an indication of pleasure.

I needed to crank it up a notch. I reached for his crotch and raked my nails over the outline of his cock, now visibly straining against the confines of his jeans. Extending the tip of my tongue and offering an abbreviated nod, I hoped he understood.

He did.

Scooting to one side of the cargo space, he angled his crotch toward my mouth.

His movements were not lost on the captain. "Everything all right back there?"

"Just getting comfortable," Tomas answered. "Should have brought a blanket, something to cover the floor."

R.J. shook his head in obvious dismissal, a silent comment on the practicalities the young sailor still had to learn.

Tomas patted his thigh, wanting my head in his lap.

I nestled between his legs. As quietly as I could, I pulled down his zippered fly. His engorged cock was not in the right position for access. There was no way I could free it from his pants.

"I'll slide over," he offered. "Give you more room." He said it for the benefit of the other men, to avoid raising suspicion over his restless shuffling.

As he lifted slightly off the floor, I shifted the fabric and reached inside his jeans. With my fingers around his cock, I looked up at him with an impish smile, wanting him to believe I was going to enjoy this as much as he would.

Setting his dick in my mouth, I felt his hand on the back of my head, the firm pressure reflecting his youthful impatience.

For the next several minutes, I sucked him slowly, letting my tongue do most of the work. Although my lips ached from resisting the ball-gag, I tried to ignore it, moving my head to provide the pleasure he craved.

It wasn't long before he was on the edge of orgasm. Feeling the twitching contractions that threatened the first spurts of cum, I took his cock deep into my mouth, letting him feel my lips against the very base of his organ.

His torso stiffened, his back arching slightly. As he pumped his thick, hot cum down my throat, I realized he'd locked his lungs, no doubt fearing the other men would realize what was happening.

I let the hot, sticky liquid find its way down naturally, not needing to force my swallow.

Although his contractions had ended, I kept my lips tight around the head of his cock. I would not release him until I had drained him completely.

I moved the last of his load into my stomach.

"Nicely done." The captain's voice broke through the drone of the road.

The possibility of his comment being directed at me sent a twinge down my spine. I hoped he was talking to Marco, complimenting him on missing a large pothole or avoiding a darting pedestrian.

I glanced at Tomas. He looked petrified, his face etched with concern. Rising from his lap, I feigned the need to stretch.

The captain and R.J. were still facing forward. That was good. There was a chance our sexual shenanigans had gone undetected.

I caught my reflection in the make-up mirror on the back of the windshield sun-shade. Wendell had flipped it down, positioning it so he could see all the way to the back of the van. The likelihood of our tryst remaining a secret was about to be exchanged for a strong dose of reality.

Even though I had remained below his direct line of vision, the dark tint of the rear glass reflected the entire area behind the seat. The combination of the mirror and the tinted glass had also given the captain and R.J. access to the show. The men had watched us from the start, when Tomas had called attention to our movements with his contrived offer to 'give me a bit more room.'

I felt like a trespasser, caught where I didn't belong. But as I looked at the cold, matter-of-fact expression on the captain's face, my guilt didn't last long. There was no suggestion of wrong-doing—in fact, he had complimented me on my skill.

Our back-seat antics had been a welcome distraction, not only for the vicarious pleasure it provided, but because the men had watched in secret, the clandestine edge adding to their enjoyment. From the Cheshire grins plastered on their faces, it looked as if watching me drain Tomas' cock had been just as satisfying as if I'd favored them personally.

Unfortunately, I had a lot to learn about reading faces.

The captain turned in his seat. "I'm sure Wendell and Marco would enjoy some of the same. Wouldn't be right, not to give them equal time. You agree, Jewel?"

The captain was showing his diplomatic side. More than providing the other men with their fair share, he wanted to reduce the importance of my focused attention on Tomas.

The idea of sucking off the other men made me ill. Perhaps they would leave me alone if I expressed a preference toward the captain— who for reasons of his own had refused to touch me from the start.

I set my chin on the seatback, my lips mere inches from the captain's face. I'd never been good at cooing, so I tilted my head slightly to the side, hoping it didn't look contrived. "It's really *your* turn."

"Thank you, but no."

The captain's refusal set off a scramble for a place in the queue.

"I'm next," Wendell said.

"But I've been doing all the driving," Marco argued. "I need a break a lot more than you do."

R.J. spoke up, siding with Marco. "Wendell, you'll take your turn last, after Marco and me. I can take over the driving for a while. Marco, pull over when you see a safe place to stop."

Maybe there was some odd, fraternal logic in Marco's argument, or R.J. saw it as an opportunity to exercise his new authority. Regardless, the order was set.

Now I would have to suck off three more men. My agreement had not been necessary— only my obedience. As far as these men were concerned, I was nothing more than a human appliance, and anyone could use me. Beyond the pleasure I could provide with my mouth or the accommodation the cavities of my body offered, I had little value.

I felt the tears welling up in my eyes. Unless God or the unlikely hand of fate intervened, I was well on my way to living a life of degradation, without any recognition that I was a woman with feelings, with my own hopes and dreams for a future.

The sound of gravel crunching under the tires jolted my senses. We were slowing, pulling off the road. Marco was ready to let R.J. take over the driving.

I didn't bother to turn around. Hearing the sound of the shift lever being driven home—the unnecessary force used to ram it into *PARK*—was a dead giveaway. Marco was anxious, ready to take his turn with me.

I felt a strange sense of abandonment as I watched Tomas rise to his knees and open the rear doors. Before jumping out to exchange places with Marco, he patted me on the bottom, letting his hand skim over my thigh.

His gesture carried a sense of gratitude laced with an apology.

Marco slid beside me, unzipping his pants. Before the four-door chorus of slamming metal subsided, he was clasping the sides of my face, pulling me toward his crotch, leaving no doubt what he wanted. And from his absolute disregard of the tears streaking my cheeks, I knew he wanted it now, without any hesitation from me.

I took several deep breaths, trying to regain control. I had to send my mind elsewhere. Because for the next few minutes, my mouth would be full as I worked to extract his jism, adding his load to the existing cum that sat heavy in my stomach.

As I slid my lips down the length of his shaft, only one thought burned within my brain. . .

Two others were waiting their turn.

Chapter Fifteen

"Buying or selling?"

We had stopped in front of a chain-link rolling gate, the only entrance into a large, unpaved parking lot. A short, scrawny Asian man was peering through the driver's window, scanning the van's interior. Wearing an old ragged shirt and baggy pants, a clipboard was his only sign of authority.

"Selling," the captain answered.

The bony little man pulled out a black marker and scrawled a number in the top corner of the windshield, then signaled to someone out of view. The gate wobbled and shook as it began to open, its erratic travel accompanied by a protest of squeaks and groans.

The Asian touched the brim of his hat. "Park other side of building. Leave cell phone in truck, like always. You need cuffs? Chain?"

"No, we're good."

The captain's voice must have jogged the gatekeeper's memory, because his jaded indifference was suddenly replaced by welcoming recognition. "Captain? That you?" The Asian stuck his head through the window, wanting a better look at the rear-seat passengers.

The captain started to answer, but the pencil-thin guard cut him off. "Ah, Mr. Captain. Very good. More business. Other one here already. Your men bring her last night."

His broken English seemed intentionally choppy, to reduce the confusing inflections of accent—and the need to repeat himself.

"She behaving?" the captain asked.

I'd been treating their conversation like an irritating background noise, not really paying attention. The captain's words finally registered. *Is WHO behaving?*

"At first, not so much. Lots of yelling. I think she wear herself out. Now sit in corner, crying. Look like shit. Not bring big money look like that."

It wasn't hard to figure out. The captain had found a second girl to sell, another unsuspecting innocent who'd refused to work the back rooms of some bar—more flesh to pay for the new boat.

I was too scared to think about it. The captain was about to put me inside a cage where men would examine me in every detail. And after they'd completed their inspection, they would put a price on not only my body, but on my very life. Whoever the other girl was, the poor thing was in the same, miserable circumstances.

The captain passed a five dollar bill into the man's waiting hands. "Same cut as before—twenty percent—right?"

The man shook his head. "No good. Need twenty-five. Big money here today."

"That's too much! More than I've ever paid. Twenty percent. That's the deal or I don't sell."

While the captain was making it clear he wasn't happy about the increased fee, from the tone of their banter, I realized the negotiation was an expected part of the process.

The Asian rubbed his chin. "You have two girls. Maybe boss say yes. I see what I can do."

The captain nodded. "Twenty it is then." He tapped Marco on the shoulder. "Drive in."

Marco over-reacted and stomped the gas pedal, spinning the rear tires on the gravel.

The lurch of the van threw me off balance, my re-handcuffed hands cracking the floor as I made an awkward scramble for support.

"Plenty of time, Marco. No need to rush," the captain said.

Yeah, Marco, no hurry. It would be a shame if I broke a wrist or a couple of fingers.

The captain hadn't thought it necessary to re-bind me with rope, but he'd insisted Tomas reapply the handcuffs as we entered the Bangkok city limits. 'More temptation requires more security,' he'd said.

Tomas pulled me tight against his shoulder, helping to steady me. He frowned and silently mouthed the word *sorry*. He'd interpreted Marco's quick acceleration the same way I did—another sign Marco was still agitated over having to resume his responsibilities as driver. For the last two hours, Marco had complained about the captain requiring the men to return to their original seating positions after I'd serviced them. He'd grumbled nonstop about Tomas's proximity giving him the advantage of being able to finger my ass or play with my tits. 'The time will pass a lot faster for him,' he'd whined. 'We should trade off, let each man take a half-hour with her.' The captain finally settled the matter with a sharp, 'Drive, Marco. Just drive.'

The exchange had given Tomas the permission—and comfort level—he needed. Although he was gentle, he was also persistent—his hands wandering over my body, cupping my ass and breasts, his fingers kneading the lips of my pussy.

But I didn't complain. It was easier to tolerate Tomas' continuous groping than to risk a change in seating companions. Tomas was the least offensive of the five men, and if tolerating his need to fondle me would limit my exposure to the others, it was a reasonable compromise.

As we drove across the lot, I took a look at the fence surrounding the entire area. Topped with a strand of barbed wire, it made a strong case for keeping out the curious and uninvited. It also eliminated the prospect of anyone on the inside from making a bolt for freedom.

In the center of the property, a huge Quonset building sat in raw, corrugated symmetry, its unpainted metal a perfect complement to the dry, dusty surroundings. Reminding me of an old airplane hangar, its ribbed surface was marred by patches of rust and the occasional dent from an errant car bumper. It gave every impression of being a long abandoned relic from some forgotten war.

The complete absence of signage made the entire place appear conspicuously transitory, a spot where the corrupt and unscrupulous could gather, immune from the interference of the more virtuous.

A small cloud of dust followed us across the lot. "Looks like they'd be making enough money to do some paving," Marco mumbled.

I wondered . . . what *are* they doing with the money?

In spite of the huge amounts of cash changing hands, the slavers had made no effort to disguise the down and dirty nature of their activities. They were content to live with the truth—their business was back-alley evil, and no amount of money could bring it out of the shadows.

Without thinking, I blurted it out. "This place is a shit-hole."

It was more than a casual observation about the real estate. I was passing judgment, condemning every man who set foot inside the gate.

The captain broke the silence. "The parking lot has been left this way on purpose."

"Because nobody likes the smell of hot asphalt in the summer?" I was pissed, and I didn't care if he knew it.

Tomas patted my leg, warning me to pull in my fangs.

"If a girl puts up a fight," the captain continued, "or tries to run, the dirt is a lot softer than paving. Does less damage."

Less damage. The men who did business here had only one priority—to protect the merchandise, keep it from getting scratched or broken. Like the skinny gatekeeper had said, it was all about the money.

"Jewel?" The tone of the captain's voice seemed odd, as if he were calling out my name while looking for me inside a crowded room.

I turned from the window to face him. "Yeah?"

"You need to listen to me." His expression carried the familiar threat of no quarter, no room for negotiation.

I realized he was waiting for a response. "I'm listening."

"The next few hours can be easy or difficult. It's up to you. If you cooperate and do as I say, you'll get through this fine. But if you put up a fight or keep the buyers from seeing the best side of you, you'll only make it hard on yourself. Understand?"

Again, Tomas was tapping my thigh, wanting me to agree.

What was I supposed to say? Arguing could bring immediate consequences—the least of which would be to restrain me in a full body-harness at the end of a thick leather leash. I had to make a good first impression on potential buyers. Entering the auction bound and shackled would mark me as combative and hostile. It was hard to admit, but it was all I had left—the hope there might be someone who would evaluate not only my physical attributes, but also my potential as a companion.

I had no choice. But before I agreed with the captain, I wanted to test my leverage, try to negotiate a promise of cooperation for increased safety.

"I have a favor to ask," I began.

The captain lifted his head.

"I'm willing to do exactly as you say. Once I'm inside that building, I'll work the buyers. I'll smile and tease them, show them whatever they want to see. In exchange, I need you to promise me something." I sounded like my mother on the night of my sixteenth birthday, when she'd told me to always use a condom even though she didn't approve of my sexual activity. "All I'm asking," I continued, "is that you don't sell me to some crazy fucker who wants to hurt me. Tell them I'm insane, or diseased, or I've got family members looking for me. Tell them anything you want, but keep the lunatics away from me."

I could tell from his expression—and thoughtful silence—I'd taken him by surprise. I hoped he was weighing my appeal with the same degree of consideration he used to evaluate any business decision.

But this was not a negotiation, and he was about to make that painfully clear.

"It doesn't work that way."

"What do you mean? You make the final decision. You control the winning bid."

He glared at me, reminding me he was the one in charge. When he spoke, his voice was stern, without a hint of compassion. "The highest bidder wins the sale. That's the way it's always been."

"But you already know which buyers are more likely to treat me like garbage," I argued. "Can't you disqualify them or something?"

His eyes narrowed. "I told you, it doesn't work that way. There's no playing favorites, no elimination of buyers unless they can't make good on their bid."

I forced out the words. "Dammit, I need your help, and I don't think I'm being unreasonable. I'll do my part, but I need to know you're not going to sell me to some crazy fucker who wants to kill me . . . *like you did with Eve.*"

It rolled out of my mouth like a witch's curse. Maybe later I would regret making a veiled threat to the man who controlled my destiny, but I was bargaining for my life and the odds were not in my favor. I had to use everything I knew.

For the longest time, the captain sat silent, his expression unchanged. Finally, he said. "It's time."

I felt a dizzy rush as the blood left my brain. I dropped my head to the back of the seat, fighting the urge to throw up, knowing there was nothing in my stomach but cum from the four men I'd sucked off. I looked up to see R.J. pulling the ball-gag from his coat pocket.

"You won't need that," I whispered. "And you might as well take these off, too." I lifted my cuffed hands. "It'll make a better impression on the buyers."

The captain motioned to R.J., directing him to put away the gag. Tomas lifted my hands toward the captain's waiting key, the metallic popping of the ratchet relieving the nagging irritation on my wrists.

With the nausea beginning to pass, I looked to the front of the van, catching my reflection in the mirror attached to the windshield visor. "Did anyone think to bring a comb or brush?"

For the first time I could remember, the captain smiled. I wondered if it was his way of saying goodbye.

Chapter Sixteen

The air reeked of cigar and cigarette smoke. And yet I welcomed it, the smothering gray haze helping to mask the pungent odor of urine and feces stabbing at my nostrils.

The captain walked next to me, close, but not touching. R.J. and Wendell shadowed us a few steps behind. I matched the captain's pace, making sure my body language was open and neutral. His agreement to remove the restraints allowed me to present myself as a submissive and obedient servant. For different reasons, we both hoped it would make me more valuable, increasing my final price.

My final price.

I was still struggling with the idea of putting a price on my head. But this place, this pig sty, is where I would be sold—to a man who would most likely treat me with no more compassion that he would his car or boat. As inconceivable as it seemed, I was about to become another asset in some wealthy man's portfolio, depreciating over time and ultimately disposable.

I put it out of my mind. I had to stay focused. Find the right buyer. Play him.

Convince him to spend the money. Then, after winning his trust, I could plan my escape.

The auction's intake area was the size of a large living room, its perimeter defined by the same chain-link fencing used to control traffic on the outside of the building. As we entered, a man wearing a necklace of keys and a thick leather belt weighted with a dozen padlocks approached the captain.

"Seen you here before, from *Kelsey* boat."

"Yes."

The man made a note on his clipboard. "Hmmm . . . this number two. You sell two girls today?"

The captain nodded.

"You know country this one?"

"American."

The man stared at my face. "Green eyes."

They exchanged a wicked glance, as if conveying secret signals in a private men's club.

"You get two numbers." He was assigning the captain lot numbers—one for me and another for the previously delivered girl. Handing the captain a stick-on badge with both numbers prominently written within the white space, he pointed to his clipboard. "Numbers good? Same as yours?"

The captain's nod wasn't enough.

The man tapped on his clipboard. "Say out loud, for sure."

"It's good. It matches."

This was not the captain's domain. His authority was limited to the representations he would make while negotiating with buyers. While inside this building, he would receive no special privileges. He would be treated the same—no better or worse—than the other sellers.

Another T-shirted staff member began waving us toward the opposite end of the enclosed area, where two huge men were waiting to pat us down. They carried no weapons, wore no uniform, and displayed no badges. But their steroid-inflated arms, bulging chests and thick, vein-studded necks conveyed a silent but effective threat. Attempting to cheat the auction out of their commission could carry fatal consequences.

Passing through the interior gate gave us access to the main part of the building, an area about half the size of a football field. An abandoned industrial warehouse would have been glamorous by comparison. While the floor-space was completely open, shafts of harsh, acrid light stretched from a series of overhead skylights to the floor, artificially segmenting the area with dingy, translucent columns of thick floating dust. Eerie and unnerving, the scene looked more like the set of a horror movie than a place of business.

Along the walls, small cargo containers sat butted together in sets of two. A short aisle-way between each set left enough room to open the doors. The fronts of the containers had been cut away and replaced with heavy gauge chain-link fencing, turning each one into a display cage. I estimated at least twenty-five sets, enough to hold fifty girls—more if they doubled up.

Many of the units were already occupied. Some of the girls hung on the wire, their fingers threaded through the chain-link, their eyes wide with confusion and anxiety. Others lie sprawled against the back walls, nearly comatose. I assumed they were under the influence of Valium or Halcion, the drugs of choice to calm the uncooperative. I wondered how many of them were victims of an unbreakable cycle of debt and desperation, strategically fashioned by their pimp-pusher, who had used violence and drugs to bend them into submission.

The newly kidnapped and indentured girls—especially those unaccepting of their fate—were immediately apparent. Pacing back and forth, they wore their scrapes and bruises like badges of honor—reminders of recent discipline.

"Those cages, they're only for girls that might run, right?" I knew the answer, but I asked anyway, hoping the captain might make an exception.

"They're called *booths*, not cages," the captain corrected me. "Before the auction starts, all the girls must be in a booth."

"But I don't need to be caged, I mean, you don't need to put me in a booth."

"Owners sit up front, at the table. We answer questions, review the bids. And before the auction can start, all the girls must be in a booth."

Even in hell, there were rules.

The building was filling with people. It was obvious who was there to buy. The window-shoppers, crewmembers, and transporters milled around in groups, chatting with each other while looking at the girls. By comparison, pimps and bar owners searching for new talent scurried from cage to cage, jotting down the lot number of their favorites. Some buyers were flanked by their own security team—obvious from the close pairings of muscular brutes moving in mirrored sync with their employers.

"What should I do first?" I asked. "Do you want me to talk to the buyers?"

"Wait until you're spoken to. The serious ones will come to you."

That seemed to be the protocol. Since entering the building, several men within eyeshot had shown blatant interest by breaking off conversations and staring at me—the white girl with the blonde hair.

The captain slowed. "I need to take my place on the platform. R.J. and Wendell will walk you to the booth."

I was hoping the captain would assign Tomas to escort me through the building, but I hadn't seen him or Marco since they'd been told to park the van and stay with the vehicle. The captain's obsession with security had eliminated any advantage I might have squeezed out of my would-be accomplice.

Wendell's hand tightened around my arm. My instinct was to pull away. Instead, I forced myself to step toward him, leaning in until our shoulders touched. His hand relaxed.

"Put 'em in together, right?" R.J. asked.

The captain stared back with scalding intensity. "Just do it," he barked.

Embarrassed, R.J. redirected the captain's anger at me. "You heard him, move your ass."

Wendell nudged me forward. "It's straight ahead and on the right."

Maneuvering through the crowd, I waited until I was sure the captain was out of earshot before pulling back.

"Keep moving, we don't have time for a pit stop." Wendell's other hand found my shoulder.

"Any chance I could see where the bidding takes place?"

The two men looked at each other, as surprised as they were confused.

"Why? What difference does it make?" R.J.'s voice was sharp and abrupt.

"I'm curious about how it works, you know, to see where the actual selling is done."

"Forget it," R.J. said. "This isn't a guided tour. You can take a look from here, and just for a second. Then into the booth."

It wasn't what I'd hoped for—I wanted to learn more about the layout, find a blind-spot or two I could use for a temporary hiding place, *if* I saw the opportunity to break free.

Disappointed, I turned toward the opposite end of the building. Even through the smoke and haze, I could see a large, raised platform set with small tables and folding chairs. Reserved for sellers, the higher perch allowed them to better see the activity—especially from buyers who intentionally remained in the background, perhaps thinking their actions were less offensive if conducted from the shadows.

R.J. tapped me on the arm and pointed toward a line of partially occupied containers. "Your booth is over there."

I didn't hesitate. But as I took the first step, I accidently let out a deep sigh, the resigned frustration too much to contain.

"You'll do fine, Jewel," R.J. said. "In a couple of hours you'll be out of here, with a new life, a new owner. Who knows what could happen."

He was trying to console me. Good god, he *was* psychotic.

As we neared the line of cages, I noticed one of them was surrounded by a congregation of men lined four deep.

"Welcome home," Wendell announced.

Noticing our approach, the men on the outer circumference gave way, creating an aisle that closed behind us as quickly as it opened. Occasionally, someone spoke—not to me, but greeting R.J. with a cautious "hello" and a simultaneous head nod. No one shook hands.

I sensed some of the men were expecting me. Assuming stares and definitive nods were as telling as flashing neon, revealing which men had been waiting to take a closer look.

I turned to R.J. "Why does the captain want you to put me in with the other girl? She could be dangerous. There are plenty of open containers. Why not use one of those?"

"Don't worry, we won't let anything happen to you. The captain thinks you'll bring more money if we put you in together, offer you as a pair."

"Like a set of bookends," Wendell added with a chuckle. "Except in this case, it's a set of pussies."

"Shut up, asshole." R.J. relished his new authority, especially when it gave him the chance to admonish a subordinate.

I was worried about my safety. R.J.'s assurances did nothing to reduce my fear of being confined with a stranger, especially if she turned out to be a drugged-out Amazon with a violent streak.

Yet, he was probably right about one thing. The captain wouldn't intentionally expose me to anyone dangerous. An injury could easily reduce my value.

"Do you know anything about her?" I asked. "Where she's from? Does she speak English?"

Both men ignored me.

"So neither of you know shit. Or is it that you don't want to tell me?"

I felt the pressure of a hand against my back. It was Wendell, adding five fingers of silent encouragement. His message was clear—*keep moving.*

I remembered when the captain first told me he was going to sell me at auction. I had naïvely imagined a human trade show, a place of opulent fantasy, where wealthy buyers would sit in leather chairs and sip expensive liquor while exotic-looking girls worked the room. I'd even imagined myself trolling from one buyer to the next, teasing them with my body to determine who would be most likely to treat me with kindness and decency. To him I would promise everything.

This was as far from silk and champagne as you could get. The auction was an ugly sideshow, an exhibition of freaks walking freely *outside* the cages, ready to engage in the most perverse and depraved activity imaginable—the buying and selling of human beings.

I tried to catch a glimpse of my cage-mate, but the men directly in front of the container were standing shoulder-to-shoulder, completely blocking the view of the interior.

Unlike the others who had given way, these men did not move. Keeping their backs to us, their attention was focused on the other girl. As Wendell and R.J. led me to the end of the container, I entered the men's line of sight.

"Look! The other one! She here! She here!"

"Better than pictures."

Pictures? Before I could put it together, before I could link circumstance with situation, the clank of the metal latch and the shrill rasp of rusty hinges focused my attention on the opening sweep of the door.

Wendell leaned in, as if expecting the girl to bolt.

"Get in," R.J. ordered. "Watch the step up, it's sharp."

I hesitated, afraid I was about to be confronted in the same way a wild animal challenges an intruding trespasser.

Wendell's hands were suddenly under my armpits, lifting me. Pushing me past the opening, he shoved me forward, the closing bang of the heavy metal door making me cringe.

Ignoring the jagged edges of cut steel, the heavy chain-link, and the filthy, bare metal floor, I scanned the space.

My first impression was one of relief. The other captive didn't look like a physical threat. Naked, she sat in the back corner, her knees drawn tight against her chest, her face buried in her folded arms. Although her hair was dark and her skin brown, the narrow tan lines around her back and bottom confirmed she was white, possibly European. Her small, shapely body made me think she was younger, but it was difficult to guess her age, especially since I couldn't see her face.

She hadn't responded to the sound of the door or the rising commotion from the men as I entered the container. Either one should have seized her attention—unless she was drugged.

As if able to read my thoughts, she raised her head.

Her eyes were swollen and red, her complexion pale, and for the longest moment, my mind refused to recognize her. She seemed to be more an apparition than real flesh and blood, as if my imagination had created a cruel illusion. But in that split second of discovery that overwhelmed the peering men, the smoky air, the stench of the filthy container . . . *I knew the truth.*

It was Annie!

She blinked her eyes. She appeared to be looking through me, my presence not registering.

She didn't recognize me.

I ached to run to her, but I held back. I had no idea what the captain or his men had done to reduce her to such a pitiful state. I had to wait until she realized I wasn't a threat—not another stranger ready to harm her.

R.J.'s voice rose up from the background chatter. "Jewel, get those clothes off."

I ignored him. I would not take my eyes off Annie.

"Jewel, did you hear me? The buyers want to see skin."

I saw a break in Annie's expression. She'd heard R.J. call out my name. She shifted her head back and forth, as if trying to focus.

Maybe she would recognize my voice. "Annie, it's me. It's Jewel. You don't have to be afraid."

She opened her mouth as if about to speak, then nothing.

"It's alright. You don't need to say anything. I want to come over there and sit next to you. Is that okay?"

Her movements were sluggish but deliberate. Very slowly, she raised an arm, extending her hand toward me.

It was all I needed. No longer concerned she might mistake me for a faceless jailor, I rushed across the container and knelt beside her, cradling her in my arms.

She finally spoke, her words little more than a faint mumble. What I heard made me shudder.

"But you're not here . . . you're dead."

She was struggling with the fact that I had suddenly appeared inside the cage, that I was still alive. She might've thought I was a hallucination, a product of her exhausted mind.

I wouldn't rush it. It was going to take time to dispel the "truth"—lies she'd been told about my death.

"New one must get naked—both of them naked."

"Clothes off. Clothes off new one."

"Must see like in picture. No fake. No fake."

More voices, all demanding, all intensely impatient.

A loud bang on the side of the container made both of us jump. I hugged Annie even tighter, determined to protect her.

"Jewel, if you don't get those clothes off, I'll have to come in there and strip you." R.J. was foaming at the mouth.

I looked up long enough to flip him off.

He stepped toward our corner. Wendell followed a few paces behind.

"Dammit, Jewel, don't make me do this." R.J. spit the words through clenched teeth. "If you force me to come in there, I'll have to make a show of it, push you down, slap you around some. It won't be pretty."

I shook my head in defiance. "Get away from us, you piece of shit."

"Let's go in," Wendell said, chomping at the bit. "You hold her down, I'll strip her."

R.J. was mumbling, his cursing growing louder. He inhaled deeply, trying to maintain control. "Jewel, listen to me," he began. "You have to take your clothes off. If you do it without being forced, the men will see you as cooperative, ready to please. There are buyers here that will notice." He hesitated a moment, then added, "Personally, I don't give a shit how it goes down. But either way, those clothes are coming off, and I mean right now!"

I didn't want them coming inside, near Annie.

I gradually began to pull away, releasing her. She tightened her grip, not understanding.

"No, Annie, I'm not leaving. I'm staying right here. I just have to get rid of these clothes."

She shook her head, her fingers sliding gently down my chest, my arms, finally grasping my hands. Her misting eyes found mine and I pressed my lips softly against hers. As we parted, I felt her body stiffen.

"It's okay. Let me stand up for a second, so I can get this dress off."

She squeezed my fingers, then reluctantly let me go.

As I rose to my feet, the noise level began to increase, the men urging me on, nudging each other in fraternal anticipation of seeing a second girl—naked—in the booth.

Keeping my eyes on Annie, I continued to offer a smile, wanting her to know we were far from beaten. She responded with a look of passive resignation, the kind of facade an innocent prisoner broadcasts to their family when execution is imminent, when all they can leave behind is a lasting memory of peaceful acceptance.

I slipped out of the dress and let it fall to the floor. Catching the oversized garment with my toes, I flipped it toward the opposite corner. Without hesitating, I slid the tiny pink panties off my hips and kicked them in the same direction.

I didn't see Annie's clothes. I hoped the captain's men had let her keep them on until the night's chill had left the building. Somehow I doubted it.

My unceremonious disrobing brought a sudden hush from the men, their heckling replaced by a sinister chorus of whispers.

"Yes, she same one. Like in picture."

"Better. Better than picture."

Returning to Annie, I dropped to my knees. Without hesitating, she reached for me, pulling me tight. Seeing our bellies touching, our breasts nestled together, brought quick and collective approval from the men. They began spurring us on, urging us to exchange more than the security of an embrace.

I brought my lips to Annie's ear. "Ignore them. They're animals."

She nodded, not ready to speak.

On the *Kelsey*, she had been my protector, keeping me safe in an unsafe world. Now it was my turn. I looked past the tears filling her eyes, determined to share what little courage I had left.

"I can't believe you're here . . . alive. I thought you were gone." My voice broke. I stopped, shaking it off. I had to control the building emotion, to stay strong for her.

I'd been sure my reunion with Annie would not take place on this earth. I had said my goodbyes. I'd reluctantly let her go. Even now, as I held her, her survival seemed as impossible as my own. Yet she was as real as the cage that imprisoned us, as alive as the bustling horde of buyers watching our every move from the other side of the wire.

Annie huddled closer, bringing her tear-streaked cheek against mine. "I . . . I was sure you were gone," she sobbed.

"I was in the water a long time. But I found a piece of wreckage and held on. A fishing boat found me the next morning."

That's all she needed to know—for now. I would tell her about Morrison, my double-crossing rescuer, later. Right now, I wanted to know how she'd survived the storm—how she ended up here, at the auction.

"The last time I saw you," I began, "you were on the stern of the *Kelsey*, holding on to the railing."

She nodded. "I found the life raft canister, but . . ." She paused, her voice quaking, her breath coming in sporadic draws.

"I know," I added. "It was empty."

She gulped, straining to get the words out. "That last wave, it was so strong. It covered the boat. I kept watching, waiting for you to surface, but . . . "

She hadn't seen me in the life raft. She had no idea R.J. had pulled me from the ocean. For all she knew, I'd been swept into the sea and drowned.

"The boat sank from underneath me," she continued. "I was in the water for a while. Finally I spotted an empty inflatable dropped by the same ship that picked up R.J. A small freighter found me the next morning." She paused. "Didn't the captain tell you?"

I shook my head. "He wanted both of us to believe the other was dead."

The captain had lied to me from the beginning. He'd kept Annie's survival a secret, knowing how his decision to betray her would affect my cooperation.

I was more than angry. He'd manipulated the truth for his benefit. He didn't care how much it hurt me, or Annie.

I had something to say, and I wanted it to reach the captain's ears. But only R.J. and Wendell were near enough to hear me. Wendell was working the crowd, talking to anyone who would listen, touting the merits of our sexual skills, while suggesting we were still a bargain at the captain's reserve price of two hundred thousand.

"R.J., you there?"

He poked his head around the corner, looking confused, not sure if he'd really heard his name.

"Yeah, I'm talking to you."

"What?" he snapped. He sensed the attention of the crowd shifting to him and he didn't like it.

"What the hell is Annie doing in this cage? She and the captain had a deal. She doesn't belong here."

"It wasn't my doing."

"Not saying it was. I'm asking you to tell me what happened between Annie and the captain after the *Kelsey* sank. I want to know why that piece of shit went back on his word."

R.J. bit his lip. I was being belligerent, and it was distracting the buyers. If it got back to the captain, R.J. would have to answer for it.

"I can't go into this right now. You need to concentrate on the men, let them get a good look at you. That was *your* agreement with the captain."

"Listen to me, you ugly cocksucker. If you don't tell me what I want to know, I'm going to throw a fucking fit right here and now. I'll scream my lungs out until one of these freaks complains to the captain. And the first question he's going to ask is why *you* couldn't handle it."

R.J.'s face flushed beet red. He was angry, and worried. Clenching his teeth in frustration, he slammed his hand against the solid end-wall of the container, a less-forgiving substitute for my face. "Jewel, someday you and I . . ."

If there hadn't been an audience to monitor his actions, I was certain he would have opened the door and beat the hell out of me.

I didn't care. What mattered is that I'd gotten through to him—and he knew I was right. This was a situation the captain would expect him to handle, especially with his new authority.

In spite of the bashing his ego had taken, R.J. reluctantly began to tell me what he knew. Even so, I had to pull it out of him—the details of who said what, the order in which it happened.

Little by little, I put the pieces together.

The pictures the captain took of Annie and I had generated a huge response from buyers. Most of them assumed we were both for sale— two young American girls sold as a set. As buyers speculated how high the bidding might go, the temptation was more than the captain could resist. Motivated by the premium he could obtain by offering us as a package, he decided to double-cross Annie and sell her— along with me—at auction. Even before the storm hit and sank the *Kelsey*, he was counting his money, anticipating his new-found fortune.

Although the loss of his ship put his scheme on hold, his intentions never changed. As far as he was concerned, he would sell one or both of us—whatever the storm returned to him.

From the moment he found Annie alive, he began encouraging buyers to attend the Bangkok auction, promising them both girls would be there. It was a marketing ploy. He knew that excited buyers brought more money and would be motivated to pay higher prices, even if only one girl was offered for sale.

Discovering I'd also survived the storm gave the captain the leverage he needed. After sending R.J. to retrieve me, he set the auction reserve at $200,000, the amount necessary to cover the insurance shortfall on replacing the *Kelsey*.

R.J.'s story confirmed what I'd suspected since my first day onboard the *Kelsey*. On the surface, the captain was strong, authoritative, and systematic. But his motivation was no different than a street pimp. When it came to the bottom line, his master was greed, and he wasn't above trading his honor and self-respect for cash.

Annie hadn't said much while I pressed R.J. for specifics. But her occasional injection of a matter-of-fact *fucker* or *asshole* told me she was listening and, in her own way, branding the captain with deceit and betrayal.

With R.J. finished, Annie added a few more of her own details. "The night of the storm, the captain pulled the memory card from his camera and stuck it in his pocket. Later, he called it an 'incredible stroke of luck.' After he found me alive, he sent those pictures out to every buyer and broker he knew, priming them for the Bangkok auction."

"But, Annie, you had a deal. The captain promised you—"

"A way out?" She finished my sentence. "Yeah, I *reminded* him of that. But after losing the *Kelsey*, he was desperate for money. He had to provision a new boat as well as cover the deductible on the insurance." She paused for a moment, to control the building emotion. "I should have known better than to trust him. But after two years, I didn't think he would turn on me—at least not like this."

The captain's treachery was unforgivable, yet as I listened to Annie, the bittersweet irony continued to haunt me—if she hadn't been rescued and returned to the captain, there was no doubt she would have died in the storm. My last sight of her had been across a gulf of raging ocean—a shadowy silhouette clinging to the stern railing of the sinking *Kelsey*. Now I wondered if finding her here, inside this filthy cage, surrounded by the most vile and despicable men on the planet, was really a better fate.

I put it out of my mind. Carl, my wretched excuse for a husband, had said it more times than I could count: *You have to play the cards you're dealt.*

It was another fucking poker metaphor, but it described our circumstances perfectly. Annie and I had drawn an empty hand, and now we had to figure out how to cut our losses to play another day.

In spite of the shit-stained floor that supported us and the rusted walls of corrugated metal imprisoning us, Annie and I had been reunited. And while the only way out of this hell was to take our chances with a stranger who would require sexual servicing, at least we would be together.

I felt the air leave Annie's chest. She pulled back far enough to look at me. "What are we going to do now?"

"We have to get through this. The best we can hope for is to find a buyer who acts half-way human, someone who won't abuse us. Then we look for weaknesses in the guy's security, find out as much as we can about the underground in the country we end up in. And when the timing is right . . . we run."

She was quiet for the longest time. Finally, she asked, "You see anyone like that out there?" Her eyes shifted to the group of men shuffling in front of the enclosure.

"I just moved in, haven't met the neighbors yet."

She smiled.

"We can do this, Annie. We'll find the right guy and play him for all he's worth. Then we'll make our move when he least expects it."

"He'll never see it coming," she added.

She was coming back to me, growing stronger, becoming more like her old self. I had no idea what the captain or his men had done to her, but the Annie I knew was strong as iron, with a will and constitution to match. Able to outwit and outsmart anyone onboard, she had intimidated the crew of the *Kelsey* into a sexual truce, threatening to poison their food if they continued to force-fuck her. She had even negotiated an agreement to keep herself out of the sex trade.

Now the captain had betrayed her, putting her right back where she was over two years ago. But Annie wasn't broken—not by a long shot. It was her nature to fight tooth and nail. She would not surrender without a struggle. And that's the Annie I needed to see. If we were going to have any influence on who bought us, she and I would have to reach deep and hold it together for a little while longer.

"Any idea how much time we have before the bidding starts?" she asked.

"One of the guys said it starts at one."

I raised my voice, wanting R.J. to hear. "Hey fuck-head, what time is it?"

R.J. banged on the side of the container. "Shut your mouth, bitch."

"Oh, is poor baby still upset?"

I waited . . . nothing.

"Okay, I'm sorry. I'll ask again, and this time with more respect. Will you please tell me what time it is, *Mr.* Fuck-head?"

Silence. I'd pushed him too far.

"We drove onto the property about eleven-thirty," I said. "I'm guessing that was an hour ago. We may have thirty minutes left."

"Got any ideas?"

I didn't, but I wasn't going to admit it. I hadn't expected this old, run-down building, and this trashy, seedy atmosphere. I'd thought men with money would want nicer surroundings, to enjoy the experience of looking and buying. Now that I'd seen the place, I wasn't sure what buyers expected.

"I think our biggest problem is the language," I said. "I don't think even half of them speak English."

"Don't let them kid you," Annie cautioned. "Most of them understand *some* English. They're just refusing to use it. They think it gives them an advantage, pretending they don't know what's going on. They'll stay with their native language until they need to make something clear, especially if it involves money."

A sudden outburst from the men forced our attention outside the container. Three rows back, several buyers were arguing with those standing in front, demanding they give others a turn at the wire.

"Maybe they'll kill each other," Annie said. "Fight it out over who gets to stand closest to the cage. That's something I'd pay to watch."

My Annie was back. And it made what I had to say easier.

"Annie, I didn't want to bring this up, but I've got a bad feeling about something."

She snorted. "Hey, we're in hell. I've got a bad feeling about a lot of things right now."

"It's more than that. On the way to the auction, one of the men let it slip there was going to be a buyer here with plenty of money, someone who'd seen the pictures of us together. I keep thinking of that guy you told me about, the one who killed your friend, Eve."

Annie's eyes narrowed, her face filling with anger. "Gregory," she hissed. "At least that's one insane bastard we don't have to worry about."

"Why do you say that?"

"We're a long way from Yangon."

"It's less than two hours by plane."

"It's not the distance, it's the politics. In Burma, he kept the local officials greased with hush money. Here in Bangkok, it's different. Unless he was able to bribe some of the government flunkies, he'd be taking a big risk crossing the border. I don't care how many bodyguards he's got, if there's a reward offered for his extradition or a contract on his head, he'd be stupid to show his face here."

Her logic made sense, but I wasn't completely convinced. "I guess it boils down to something the captain said. Actually, it has more to do with what he didn't say."

She shrugged her shoulders. "What?"

I heard the irritation in her voice. I'd forgotten how tired she was. I'd tell her what I knew and then drop it. There was no point pushing her into an argument.

"I confronted the captain about Gregory. I told him I knew about Eve, and who killed her. I didn't mention Gregory by name, but I might as well have. Then I told the captain I was willing to play up to the buyers to push the prices up, but only if he promised not to sell me to the same psycho."

Annie's eyes grew wide with surprise. "The hell you did! I wish I'd been there to see it."

"It just came out. I was scared and he wasn't giving an inch. I thought I could use it as leverage."

She thought for a moment. "It didn't work, did it?"

Annie knew the captain better than I did. Assuming he would restrict his business activities—and his compensation—had been a stupid mistake.

"He didn't answer me," I said. "He let the question hang there, pretty much made it clear he didn't care who bought me or what happened to me after the auction."

"The fucker would sell his own daughter if the price was right."

I nodded. "The more I think about that conversation, the more I ask myself why he didn't lie to me. You know, to pacify me, keep me calm. Whether he knew or not, he could have told me Gregory wasn't going to be here."

I was beginning to feel the same trepidation, the stomach-churning anxiety that had sent me racing to the toilet that last night on the *Kelsey*.

Annie blew a puff of air toward her forehead. The place was heating up and she was starting to sweat. She pulled away from me enough to let the air circulate between us.

"I still don't think there's much of a chance of Gregory showing up," she said. "But if it makes you feel better, Massey told me there's a way to identify him. It has to do with his eyes. The men who've seen it say it's a dead giveaway."

"His eyes?"

"They're cloudy and dull, without color. Like someone with cataracts."

"He's going blind?" My voice was dripping with hopeful expectation.

"It's a rare eye disease. Forces him to wear really thick glasses. The lenses look like the bottom of a Coke bottle."

I tried to imagine what a spec-wearing, cloudy-eyed nerd with a penchant for killing young girls with electricity might look like—maybe a character out of an old Hitchcock or Wes Craven movie.

"What if he's wearing contacts?"

"Can't use them. Supposedly it has something to do with the disease."

"So we stay away from anyone wearing Coke-bottle glasses with eyes that look like a shit-pit."

"In a nutshell . . . yeah."

Chapter Seventeen

"Look at the tits on that one. Wanna put my hands on those."

"Tiny holes, tight. Good for fucking."

Crude and impersonal judgments. Rude and offensive remarks. For a moment, I ignored them. Then I remembered our situation. Our bodies were being evaluated by men who were there to *buy us*. Their purchase criteria was based on our physical characteristics. Unfortunately, it was from that same group of men we hoped to find one who would treat us with kindness rather than cruelty. And that man would make his decision to bid—or pass—based on what we did next.

Onboard the *Kelsey*, Annie had taken care of me. Now it was my turn. My goal was to find a buyer who would promise two things: He would not separate us, and he would agree to treat us humanely.

I shut my eyes, needing that instant of darkness to transform myself.

Smile. Walk toward the front of the cage, let them look. Show them what they want to see.

I looked out at the sea of faceless men. I had to approach them with the same objective as any professional salesperson—presenting myself to the best advantage. Features and benefits. Fantasy and anticipation. These were the tools of influence and persuasion.

Although it was difficult to see beyond the first two rows of heads, I guessed the crowd to be about fifty or sixty strong. Mostly Asians, East Indians, and Europeans, the languages were just as varied—Russian, Thai, and Chinese. There were others I couldn't identify.

I needed to separate the real money from the gawkers and working stiffs. I scanned the men in the front row. Assuming buyers would be better dressed, I decided to ignore anyone wearing thread-bare or ill-fitting garments.

I took my first step toward the wire, then watched in amazement as the men mimicked my actions, leaning forward in unison. Those in front grasped the chain-link with their fingers, unwilling to surrender their coveted position—and the privileges it offered.

I took another step, letting my fixed smile evolve into a pouty grin. The men's demeanor began to change, their boisterous, juvenile obsession with nudity replaced with quiet smiles of anticipation.

REUNION

It reminded me of a Sunday morning congregation of hopeful souls, their spontaneous and happy chatter giving way to a hushed silence as the minister climbed the steps to take his place behind the podium—except this crowd was not waiting for a sermon. This audience was far removed from the hereafter, and I doubted any of them were still in possession of a soul.

I needed a way to talk to them one at a time to determine which buyer offered the advantages of preferred treatment. Until I knew which man to favor, I had to keep as many of them engaged as possible.

I was three steps away from the front of the cage. The men began beckoning me forward, encouraging me to press myself against the chain-link. They wanted to touch me with their fingers, now anxiously extended through the wire like a squirming wall of stubby tentacles, all eager for contact. There was no question they wanted to penetrate me.

This was not the time to waver or show any hesitation. Seventy sets of eyes were watching every move, every expression. Evaluating. Assessing. Calculating how much they would pay.

"Both of us," I said softy. "If you want these," I slid my hands over my breasts, squeezing them, "you need to buy both of us."

Disappointment swept their faces.

They didn't want to be teased. They wanted to handle the merchandise.

I had tried to negotiate much too early in the game. They were losing interest.

I took another step, winking at several men in the front row, suggesting the promise of doing business on their terms.

Their wary expressions began to fade.

I widened my stance, letting them see. Keeping my eyes on the gawking men, I separated the lips of my pussy, showing them the pink interior, hoping it would be enough.

Several men began drawing small circles in the air, the universal signal for turning around. I was surprised, not because they wanted to see the rest of my body, but because I had actually connected with them. Before approaching the wire, the majority had stared at me as if I were a sideshow freak, their comments purposely directed at each other. Now, a half-dozen of them were communicating with the naked girl in the cage. I nodded confidently, my mouth parting into a faux smile before turning to present my backside.

Knowing they expected to see it all, I spread my legs wide and slowly bent over. Rotating my hips, I turned to the right, then the left, giving all of them the same view.

An unexpected bump against my head almost toppled me. I'd been focused on the dirty steel floor, and Annie's approach took me completely by surprise. Our hands momentarily floundered in a soft collision as we reached for each other.

"Don't move," she whispered. "Stay right there."

She had come to join me, to raise the level of interest—and the price. She knew how important it was to eliminate the pimps and club owners from the competition. They would think nothing of splitting us up. If we could show the wealthy bidders how much more valuable—and fun—we were as an inseparable pair, we could increase the odds of staying together.

I nestled my head against Annie's stomach. She reached over my back, her hands finding my bottom. Grasping each butt-cheek, she spread me open.

The men responded with *oohs* and *ahhs,* followed by mumbles of approval. A few of their comments were in English.

"Small, very small. Yes, yes, very good."

"Tiny hole, like doll. Look! Very tight!"

In a world where physical desirability was measured in dollars and cents, their crude comments might be considered compliments—their praise of my physical anatomy a positive financial assessment. But right now, my only purpose was to raise the bar, with the intention of out-pricing the pimps and back-room brokers. I would consider their observations in the same way they'd been offered—strictly business.

"Try to look at them," Annie said, breaking through the low-spoken chatter of the men. "Bend down a bit and look back at them through your legs. Establish eye contact with as many as you can."

I did as she suggested, trying to appeal to what little humanity might still exist in this perverse and insane world where the buying and selling of human beings was as common as picking out fresh fruit at the market.

"Come closer!"

"Here! Bring here, closer!"

I'd hoped showing the men every crevice and cavity of my body would be enough.

It wasn't.

Putting their hands on the merchandise—making physical contact—was part of the process. If I balked or ignored them, I could easily discourage the very bidders I hoped to attract. Somewhere in that throng of crazy perverts, there had to be at least one man with a thread of compassion and the financial resources to buy us both.

I realized their demands for a personal inspection were directed only at me. What about Annie? Certainly the men expected to see her body as well as mine pressed against the wire.

I didn't get the chance to ask. Annie pulled me in as I stood upright, my back toward the men.

"This is the hard part," she said. "A few will want to feel your skin, pinch you, twist your nipples. But most of them will want to put their fingers inside you. It's how they test you, to see if you're willing to let them use your body any way they want." Annie hesitated, letting her eyes drop to the floor. Then she added, "And it's not going to be quick."

Now I understood. She had already taken her turn—or been forced to—earlier, before I was placed in the cage. She had endured the swarm of penetrating fingers alone.

Now, many of those same fingers waited for me.

A scarce eighteen inches remained between me and the front of the cage. I took a step, reducing the distance by half.

"Yes, yes, closer, come closer."

"Over here. Waiting here for you."

"Against wire. Bring pussy here."

I inched forward, looking at the faces, trying to determine which man would be less aggressive, which one might show the others how to be gentle, probing without hurting me.

I stopped short of the chain-link, but near enough to let the quivering ribbon of anxious digits finally make contact. The men produced a collective *ahhh* as the tips of their fingers brushed against my skin.

There was nothing left now, no gambit to play, no reason to delay the inevitable.

Closing my eyes, I pressed my body against the wire.

Chapter Eighteen

"You know rope? Leather? You know how make sex with leather?"

Another buyer, making conversation.

Annie and I made our evaluations on the spot, casting our vote with a clandestine tap on the other's butt when in agreement. Those buyers passing our initial and admittedly superficial test of appearance received our attention. In determining how they planned to treat us, one of us would respond with a smile, the other with words. Then leaning close to the wire, always holding each other, always caressing each other, we would offer compliments on the way he was dressed or how his eyes or hair was one of his best features. Each responded with little-boy enthusiasm. Often surprised at our willingness to interact with them, many leaned in against the cage, ignoring the galvanized metal wire as it pressed against their foreheads.

"So what about it, baby? You trick with leather?"

Annie shook her head, then turned to me and let out a forced laugh. It was an insult, meant to emasculate and embarrass the sadists and serial abusers. We knew it was a risk. It would either prevent them from bidding or make them determined to buy us, if only to extract their revenge. But we had no choice—simply ignoring them would give us far worse odds.

Wendell had continued to hover right outside the cage, and although he didn't try to control or influence our conversations with the men—any interference on the part of a seller could be interpreted as an effort to hide a girl's defective personality or attitude—he continued to bring attention to the "pair of white girls" for sale. Waving buyers over, he would start the conversation with "two girls, pretty, pretty." Holding up two fingers, he added, "licky-licky," then smacked his lips. At first, I thought he was touting our skills of fellatio. I quickly learned he was referring to our willingness to go down on each other.

After an hour of "barking" at the crowd, Wendell approached us. "We need to build some excitement, get the buyers talking about you, you know, the way they did when we first threw you together. Why don't you two fuck each other?"

Annie fired back, her voice syrupy sweet. "Aww, Wendell, you know there's nobody we'd rather fuck than you. Oh, wait! I forgot. Your dick doesn't work anymore, not since that girl in Phuket stabbed it with a fondue fork. Remember, honeypot?"

Wendell's face turned hot crimson. "Go fuck yourself, Annie." Too embarrassed to fight back, he turned and disappeared into the haze-covered crowd.

"Any of that true?"

Annie nodded. "Wendell worked aboard the *Kelsey* last year. On one of our runs, we did an overnight in Phuket. Wendell got drunk and tried to stick his dick up a working girl's ass while she was asleep. The girl grabbed a fondue fork and chased him up six flights of stairs. The exertion, on top of the booze, forced him to stop at one of the landings to puke. While he was hanging his head over the side, the girl came up from behind and rammed the fork between his legs. Caught part of his balls and grazed his cock."

I winced, then started to laugh. For a moment, my mind had wandered outside the cage—and it felt good. To anyone else, our casual chat about a pissed off working girl getting her revenge by skewering Wendell's testicles would have sounded perverse and twisted. But to us, it was girl talk—a bloody fondue fork taking the place of lipstick and shoes.

Without Wendell's prying eyes and ears, I could speak freely. There were a thousand questions I wanted to ask Annie—everything from how long she'd been in the water after the *Kelsey* went down, to how she'd been treated since the captain found her.

I never had the chance.

"You're very pretty. Don't see many like you. At least not here, at the auction."

He was young, probably late twenties. Wearing tan pants and a light blue shirt, he looked presentable, but not affluent. In contrast to his clothes, his longish dark hair was precision cut and perfectly styled, reflecting the constant care of a custom barber. Of average looks and build, he seemed approachable and friendly. I noticed his watch—a two-tone TAG Heuer. Nice, but it lacked the financial statement of a Rolex.

I decided to give him the benefit of the doubt. With this crowd, leaving expensive jewelry at home made more sense than risking a blow to the back of the head delivered by a two-bit thief.

I moved to the wire and set my legs at shoulder width, letting him see as much as he wanted. I waited for him to glance down, but he kept his eyes—I noticed they were mismatched in color—centered on mine.

"Hi, I'm Jewel. You a local boy?"

"Nobody's local, sweetheart. This is the most outta town crowd you're ever gonna meet."

He was American, the slang giving him away.

"You bought girls before?" Annie asked. "I mean, from the auction."

He hesitated, his guard rising. "Why do you ask? Is that important?"

Annie wrapped one arm around my waist and brought the other hand to my chest, playfully cupping my right breast. "It's our first time, and frankly, we're a little freaked. If you could tell us what to expect, it might help."

She was backpedaling, trying to get him to open up, tell us something personal.

"I've never bought before, but I like to window-shop." He turned his head slightly, the light catching a diamond ear stud in a kaleidoscopic flash of color.

There was something more to this man than his appearance. I wondered if Annie sensed it, too. His conversation, mannerisms, even his body language conveyed a comfortable, almost casual acceptance of everything around him. I had the feeling he'd been here plenty of times, and he'd done a lot more than look.

"Do you know the man who's selling us?" I asked. "Everybody calls him the captain." I was reaching, attempting to find something in common.

"Not really." He shrugged his shoulders. "I might recognize him if I saw him. But I don't recall ever having a real conversation with him."

Not really? Might? A real conversation?

He was lying. Not only was his face twitching like a lizard's tail, he'd contradicted himself three times. My asshole, poker-playing husband had taught me to recognize the signature giveaways—the signs of a bluff—when teaching me the finer points of the game.

I tapped Annie on the butt, then swished my fingers back and forth, hoping she understood. We needed to push him, get more information—find out if he had the money to compete with the high-rollers, and most important, if he would he treat us humanely.

"Yeah, the captain thinks we make a sweet pair," I said, giving Annic a loud smack on the cheek. "Is that what you're looking for, a set of two?"

He turned his head and squinted at me. "Not sure yet."

Another twitch, this time Annie saw it too. She pinched my bottom to acknowledge it.

When first approaching us, he seemed indifferent over the fact we were naked. Now he was looking us over in earnest, his eyes racing back and forth between our breasts and pussies, not caring that his actions were obvious.

I wanted to ask him straight out: *Are you a buyer? Do you have two hundred grand in your pocket? Just tell us . . . yes or no.*

Perhaps he had his reasons for being elusive. Some men—especially an American— would want to stay under the radar, keep their intentions confidential. We had no choice. Until we knew his financial status and his intentions to bid, we had to keep up the suggestive patter.

Annie began sucking on her middle finger, coating it with spit. Withdrawing it from her mouth, she set it between my legs. "Anything we can do to convince you to take us home with you? We promise we'll be lots of fun if you keep us together."

Thrusting my hips forward in mock desire, I separated my legs even more, encouraging Annie to slide inside. She got the message.

The sudden rise in his chest was a good sign—better than any lie detector. We would break down his defenses with a cocktail of testosterone and adrenaline.

"I don't know if I can afford this kind of action," he said with caution. "You two are damn hot, probably push the bidding way up."

That was the first thing he'd said that was promising. Now we had to motivate him, do whatever was necessary to get him to the bidder's table. We'd seen nothing obvious that could be interpreted as a physical threat. And as far as I knew, he was the only American who'd approached our cage. By comparison, an American would most likely treat us better than men raised in cultures where women were automatically disadvantaged by their gender.

Another man joined him at the wire. The cherub-faced Asian had been watching at a distance and grown curious about the apparent mutual interest between us and the young buyer.

Concerned it might distract our mark, I flicked my fingers at him. "Shoo. Go away. We're busy."

Understanding enough English to get the gist of what I was saying, he frowned, glared back at me, then walked away.

"Let's keep this to the three of us," I said. "We don't need some nosey twit with a peanut-sized cock trying to horn in."

The change in his expression told me he got it—I had expressed a preference . . . for him.

"Speaking of cock . . ." Annie let her words hang for a second, then added, "I'll bet yours is really nice." She was working him, getting ready to set the hook. Turning to me, she said, "What do you think, lover? Would you like to see his cock?"

I answered with a breathless whisper. "I really would."

He licked his lips, his tongue unconsciously telling us he liked what he was hearing.

Annie pulled her fingers from my pussy and brought them to her lips. Licking them clean, she pulled my mouth to hers, wanting to share. As we separated, she said, "I'd like to *taste* his cock."

He swallowed hard, his face flushed.

We had him.

I motioned to Annie, to make sure she saw his raging boner straining against the loose fabric of his khaki slacks.

"I . . . like you both," he stammered. "But buying you together, it's going to take a lot of money." He began to back away.

"Hey, where are you going? Come back here." Annie motioned to him with a wave of rippling fingers.

It was time to close the deal, to convince him to take us both—at any price. And there was no better way to motivate him than to exploit the storm brewing between his legs. If we could keep him within reach, Annie and I could touch him, or let him touch us.

He took another step backward.

"Is it something we said?" Annie kept trying, wanting a response.

I decided to be more direct. "Get your ass back here. We're ready to get up close and personal with you. You can't leave us now."

He shook his head, a roguish smile on his lips. "I'll, ah . . . I'll be back." He turned and retreated into a shaft of dusty float suspended from an overhead skylight.

"Crap. He doesn't have the money. Probably not even a real buyer." I sounded like we had just missed the ice cream truck.

"Maybe, but I got the impression he was telling the truth when he said he'd be back."

I hoped she was right. It was too much out of character for any man—at least any straight man—to cut short a sexy conversation with two naked females.

"He might need to transfer some funds, or want to talk to the captain about buying us outright." I was rationalizing his quick exit.

Annie was squinting, peering through the haze of cigarette smoke. "Hmmm, I'm not sure, but that could be him over there talking to R.J." She pointed to a group of silhouettes standing about fifty feet away. "Look toward the middle of the building."

Even through the garish light and eclipsing shadow, I recognized his profile. Characterized by his longer, highly-styled hair, he stood out from the rest of the crowd. Deep in conversation with R.J., he was nodding, his entire body rocking back and forth.

I noticed two muscled heavy-weights standing to the side, monitoring the activity around the American.

Bodyguards.

The stakes had just changed. If he could afford a private security team, he had plenty of money. And he was here to do business.

R.J. glanced up at the ceiling, as if he'd been asked a question and was searching for the answer somewhere on that dirty half-moon of galvanized metal.

Even through the smoky haze, I could see our young admirer digging in his pants pocket. "What's he doing?" I asked. "Playing with himself?"

Annie didn't respond.

"Maybe he's looking for his checkbook, to make a deposit," I offered.

"Nobody does business with a check. Not here." Annie's voice was full of nervous caution. "It's all done with cash or a wire transfer."

Whatever the American had pulled from his pocket was now the subject of their conversation. R.J. looked down at the contents of the man's extended hands. Tipping his head as he accepted the items, it appeared they had come to some kind of agreement.

That made no sense. As far as I knew, R.J. had no authority to bargain on behalf of the captain. Even if he did, the bidding wasn't done that way. The captain had told me all buying and selling took place at the front of the building. Sellers waited on the raised platform, ready to negotiate offers when their lot number was called. That's the way it was done. *No exceptions*, he'd said.

Even with the captain's explanation, the exchange between R.J. and the young buyer made me uneasy. "You think we did the right thing? You know, encouraging him?"

Annie shrugged her shoulders. "He's American. That's the best set of credentials we could hope for. These foreign bastards wouldn't think twice about sitting on our face and using our tongues for toilet paper. We had to go with our gut."

The mental picture of lying on my back while cleaning some camel-jockey's asshole made me cringe. But Annie was right. Encouraging *any* buyer was risky, but sitting back and doing nothing left us dependent on the luck of the draw. And from the looks of the crowd, the odds were less than promising.

R.J. and the young American began walking toward us. R.J.'s hands hung at his sides, his fingers closed in loose fists.

"Whatever the guy gave R.J. must be pretty important," I said. "He's got one in each hand, and he's holding on to them like they're made of gold." I thought for a moment. "Could that be it? A couple rolls of gold coins to use as a deposit?"

Annie's eyes fixed on the advancing men. "I . . . don't . . . think so."

The buyer stopped about ten feet from the cage, letting R.J. approach us alone.

I stepped to the side, making sure the American knew I was talking to him. "Hi, sweetie. Back for a second look?"

Annie followed my lead. "We missed you. You been off making plans for the three of us?"

He ignored our questions. Compared to our earlier flow of easy chit-chat, he was distant and aloof. And for some reason, he wanted R.J. to do all the talking.

For several seconds, both men just stood there—R.J. at the front of the cage, and the American ten feet behind—staring at us. Although not meant to be a challenge, I realized we were returning their gaze. And it was becoming uncomfortable.

Annie broke the silence. "Hey stud, what's up? You lost your voice?" She wasn't pulling any punches. She wanted a response from the suddenly unsociable buyer.

R.J. looked back at the American. The young buyer nodded at him, then gestured toward Annie and I, apparently reminding him of the possibility of a sale.

Still reluctant, R.J. kicked at the ground, as if not sure how to begin. Now I knew something was up. I'd never seen him hesitate to speak his mind.

Finally he dropped his head, unwilling to meet our eyes. "This guy tells me you had quite a conversation."

"And?" I was pushing, wanting the bottom line.

"He's interested in seeing how you handle some of his toys. He wants you to wear them, to put them in."

213

Annie bristled. "Put them in? What the fuck are you talking about?" She was tired of being messed with, and she wasn't going to mince words. "Show us," she demanded.

R.J. opened both hands, palms up.

Annie recognized the objects immediately. "Shit. He saw the pictures, didn't he?"

It took me a moment to realize what R.J. was holding—two polished stainless steel butt plugs. "That's what he wants?" I asked. "To see us with those *things* up our ass?"

"He won't bid unless you show him, like in the pictures."

I felt Annie's chest expand and contract. Confined to the cage since last night, she'd had little or no sleep. She'd already endured more than her share of poking and prodding.

I pulled her to me, the momentary distraction of our breasts sliding together not enough to dispel my concern over the buyer's need to distance himself. "Could be a test," I whispered. "To see how we react, how submissive we'd be as sex partners."

R.J. raised his voice. "Hey! Are you two listening? I need both of you to put these in." He'd returned to his usual arrogant self and was flaunting his authority in front of a

214

prospective buyer, trying to emphasize his own importance.

"Back off, asshole," Annie shot back. "Tell your boy we're thinking about it."

She brought her lips to my ear. "I need a second," she whispered. "I'm so tired of being fucked with." She paused. "But you're right. We can't cut this guy loose too soon."

R.J. forced a smile and turned to the buyer. "No problem. They're deciding on the best position, so you can see everything."

In spite of R.J.'s show of bravado, we'd heard the bottom line: This squeaky-clean kid wasn't going to bid on us unless he could see Annie and I posed with the plugs in our butts.

I stepped back from the wire. My heart was pounding, my breath coming in short, shallow drafts. I had no idea why the buyer's request was making me so anxious. I'd done other things—much more degrading things—than this. He simply wanted to see a live re-enactment of the photographs the captain had taken on my last night aboard the *Kelsey*.

I reached for Annie. "Why is this making me so nervous?"

She shook her head. "It's the way he's asking, treating us like objects. On top of that, he's using R.J. as a mouthpiece, refusing to approach us directly." She squeezed my arm, trying to reassure me. "I don't like it any more than you do, but if we want to keep the kid interested . . ."

Annie understood our predicament as well as I did. We were in no position to argue. This guy might be the one with enough money to keep us out of the hands of street pimps and bar owners. He also seemed to understand our desire to stay together. If sticking a pound of stainless steel up our asses would motivate him to buy us as a set, it would be a small price to pay.

R.J. leaned in, whisker-close to the chain-link. "Well? You two gonna do this or do I need to get some of the crew?"

It was an empty threat. He didn't dare discipline us in front of a buyer. It would make us appear hard to control, stubborn, and argumentative—just the opposite of what he wanted to convey. His problem was personal. Our continuing hesitation was making him look bad in front of a buyer, and he didn't like it.

Annie intentionally emphasized the sway of her hips as she turned away from R.J. and toward the buyer. She wanted both men to know she was talking only to our potential benefactor. "What's the matter, handsome? Lose your tongue?"

Her voice carried the vampy lilt of a seductress, her body language open and honest. Annie was exhausted, but her mind was still razor-sharp. She was re-establishing contact, making him understand we would do it for *him*. Our performance would be a show of favoritism, our actions reflecting our expectations of him paying the price—*for both of us.*

The buyer began to fidget, shifting his weight. Annie had struck a nerve. She'd called him out, refusing to let him hide behind the make-believe wall he'd thrown up. Now he had to decide whether to stay or run.

"I need to hear you say it," Annie continued. "Tell me you want it. Tell me how much you want to see it. We'll do anything you want. All you have to do is ask."

He rubbed a finger over his bottom lip. He was hesitating. Finally, he cleared his throat and said, "I want to see it." His voice was no louder than a stage whisper.

"Tell me, sweetheart," Annie coaxed. "What do you want to see?"

"I want to see you put the plugs in your ass."

"And you'll watch us? Promise you won't take your eyes off us for a second?"

"Not for a second."

Even in these miserable circumstances, Annie could be clever, sexy, and manipulative. And while her antics might seem to be nothing more than playful flirtation, she had persuaded the buyer to treat us as people, not puppets. He would pay much more for us if he saw us as willing companions, ready to please him.

R.J. was struggling to push the plugs through the chain-link. "I can't get them through the wire. I'll have to open the door." He motioned toward the opposite end of the container. "Both of you, get your asses to the other end of the booth and stay there."

We turned toward R.J. with simultaneous, almost synchronized motion that couldn't have looked better if we'd rehearsed it. "We'll do it for you, 'cause you asked so nicely," Annie said.

"And we won't move a muscle," I added.

The raspy squeak of the door hinges was like setting off a security alarm, interrupting conversations and arresting the attention of buyers a hundred feet away.

In his haste to set the plugs inside the cage and reclose the door, he dropped one of them, tried to recover it, then gave up as it rolled across the steel floor. Frustrated, he slammed the door shut, forcing dozens to cringe as the loud metallic clang echoed throughout the building.

It was good to see him rattled. His new responsibilities weighed on him like thirty pieces of cursed silver. And like Judas, I hoped he would come to the same ugly end.

I retrieved the plugs and handed one to Annie. About four inches long, they were of similar design to the one I'd worn for the captain—a flared bud with a narrow stem. But instead of the base adorned with colored glass or Swarovski crystal, it was plain, flat metal.

"Let's get this over with," I whispered.

She shook her head. "No, I'll take the first one."

Without hesitating, Annie dropped to all fours and pointed her butt toward the crowd.

Kneeling beside her, I began to caress her bottom, thinking it was what the buyer would want to see.

"Slide the plug up and down my crack," Annie instructed.

The buyer began moving to the front of the container. He obviously wanted a show. And now, Annie and I would give him one, slowly building his expectations, letting him relish the moment when I finally pushed the plug deep into Annie's ass.

Our actions were generating a new wave of interest. A dozen men clamored toward the cage. Then twenty more crowded in, all pushing and shoving to claim a coveted position at the front. I looked at the buyer and grinned, wanting him to understand that no matter how many other men were watching, we were doing this *only* for him.

Maybe he saw the gesture, maybe not. The other men jostling around the cage were distracting him, their hyper-activity and growing chatter reflecting their eagerness to see Annie and I engage each other. But after a few seconds, I realized he didn't appear to mind the commotion. In fact, his growing catty smile told me he was enjoying it.

I realized the truth—he considered the commotion from the other men as confirmation of our desirability. In a world where men constantly sought the approval of others, the clamor outside the cage was a strong indicator of our value as potential possessions. For this socially stunted man-child with a two-hundred-dollar haircut, buying pretty things was more than a pretentious and superficial pastime. It was his way of invoking the envy of other men. Even when his eyes returned to Annie's bottom, he remained intensely aware of what was going on around him.

I hated his arrogance.

Yet, he was, in every sense, in charge.

Separating Annie's cheeks brought looks of delight from the men. While I anticipated the smiles, I wanted to laugh at those with gaping mouths, as if they were trying to taste her from a distance.

Tapping the tip of the plug against her smallest hole brought audible panting from many, their tented trousers confirming their single-minded obsession.

Without looking up, Annie asked, "Are the bastards insane yet? Make them wait for it, until they're ready to come in their pants." Her initial frustration over having to tolerate more probing—this time with a piece of machined steel—had been replaced with purposeful intent.

I swept the small of her back with my left hand. "Wish we had a mirror so you could see."

Annie cocked her head to the side, straining to glimpse the sea of faces. The sight struck her as I hoped it would, evoking a bit of pathetic humor. "My God, it looks like feeding time at the zoo."

Turning toward the anxious men, I placed the silver bulb in my mouth and twirled it for several seconds, then opened my lips to let them see me work my tongue over the bright metal.

The men had continued talking nonstop, some commenting to each other, others spouting impulsive spurs, goading us on. Bringing the plug to Annie's puckered hole evoked a sudden and near-ethereal hush from the crowd. No one spoke—no one moved—for fear of missing the moment of penetration.

"Okay, hold it against me." Annie pressed back against the tip, taking it in slowly, stretching her opening to accommodate the toy's full circumference. As she passed the widest part, the plug seated easily, leaving the flat, circular base tight against her bottom.

Annie swished her hips back and forth, flexing her butt muscles in simulated delight. "Ooh, that feels so good," she crooned, her mocking dialogue lost on the drooling men.

It was my turn. But the process seemed mechanical, and I wasn't sure how much ceremony—if any—should be part of the performance. "Now what?" I whispered. "Do we trade positions?"

"Not yet. We've got their attention, so let's work it to our advantage."

Annie squeezed her butt-cheeks, the contractions making the gleaming metal cap rise and quiver. I resumed my exaggerated caressing of her tight, shapely ass.

"Oh, yes, yes," she moaned. "Press on it, push it in deeper." It was beyond dramatic, and I heard her stifle a chuckle.

Her feigned pleasure had an obvious effect on the men. Some turned to each other in shared amazement while others spontaneously mumbled their approval in their native language.

I looked around for the American buyer.

He was leaning against the container, off to my right.

Abandoning his previous façade of a cold and detached stoic, he was watching intently, his Cheshire smile telling me he was more than satisfied. As his eyes found mine, I winked.

He pointed at me, mouthing the words, *your turn.*

"Annie, our all-American boy-toy is at the front of the cage. He wants to see a matched set."

"Well, bless his heart and kiss my ass."

She was being sarcastic, but I couldn't help myself. I left a quick kiss on her bottom, then turned to face our potential new owner. "Can you see okay? I don't want you to miss anything."

He gave me a haughty, self-important lift of his head, obviously pleased with the personal attention.

On all fours, I scooted forward next to Annie until our butts were side-by-side. "Want to try it from here?"

"Yeah, let's give the little fucker a show. Ready?"

A part of me was hesitating. But putting it off wasn't an option. We were making a sales pitch, and stopping in the middle of our presentation could end any possibility of closing the deal.

Annie held the second plug between her fingers and tested her reach. "I can't get to you from here. You need to scoot up a bit."

I crawled forward a couple of hand-lengths. "Okay, now try it."

Annie swirled the bulb in her mouth and reached back, probing at my butt with the smooth metal tip. The awkward stretch still had her fumbling.

"This isn't working," she said. "I have to see what I'm doing. You stay put."

On her knees, she turned toward the men and brought her face close to my bottom. Taking her time, she caressed each cheek, leaving a kiss here and there as she streaked my skin with her tongue.

"You should see these morons," she said. "Their eyes are about to pop out of their heads."

"What about the buyer?"

"Oh, yeah. He's in a fucking trance."

Annie set the pound of polished steel between my cheeks and pressed the tip against my opening. Feeling the resistance, she hesitated. "You're tight as hell. You've got to relax, otherwise it's going to hurt."

I'd been concentrating on loosening the muscles in that part of my body since dropping on all fours. But my torso felt like it was wrapped with steel cables. The men, the cage, the anxiety over what the next hour would bring, was keeping my asshole locked as tight as a bank vault.

I gritted my teeth. "Just push it in and get it over with. My knees have had it with this metal floor."

The burning sting of insertion forced all my attention to the point of contact. I sucked in the air, trying to reduce the aching discomfort. I didn't care that the men at the front of the cage heard it, especially after their snorted grunts suggested a strong sadistic streak resided within their collective libidos.

Annie gave a final push and seated the plug. "That okay?"

"Yeah. Stings a bit, but I can live with it."

"Huh. I wonder what this is?"

I assumed she'd found a new bruise on my bottom, or an old one turning color. "It's from the floor of the van," I said. "I didn't have the most comfortable seating arrangements on the way here."

"That's not what I'm talking about. This little hole . . ."

"That's right," I interrupted. "And now this little hole is full. So let me wiggle my ass for a minute so I can get off this floor. My knees are killing me."

"Hush. You don't understand. Stay put for a minute." I felt her fingernails scratching across the base of the plug. "Did you look at the bottom of these things? There's a hole in the center."

"So?" The feeling of Annie's thumb sliding back and forth over the exposed end of the plug was not unpleasant, but unappreciated under the circumstances.

"And there's something stamped next to it, a symbol of some kind, but I can't make it out."

The men against the wire were talking again, those speaking English making comments about how they wished the plugs were bigger, to see how we would accommodate a larger-than-average-sized cock. Others were asking us to come closer, to press our bottoms against the chain-link so they could grasp the plugs and work them in and out.

We ignored them. Neither of us wanted to risk irritating our potential buyer by responding to anyone but him. Even without his influence, I didn't want some insensitive jerk doing an exploratory in my asshole.

"Maybe it's part of the design," Annie said. "You know, for mounting it on a display rack."

"Could be."

Whatever Annie found intriguing about the plug's construction had failed to pique my interest. I just wanted to get off the floor.

"What about the one inside me?" Annie asked. "Is it the same, with a small symbol off to the side?"

"I don't remember a symbol, but I think the hole was there. I felt it when I pushed it in."

Reaching between her legs, Annie felt for the protruding base of the plug. "Yeah, I feel it. It's not as worn as yours." She paused, drawing in a couple of noisy breaths. "I need to see it."

Something about the plugs was bothering Annie. I had no idea what, but it was important enough to bring our performance to an abrupt end.

Still on her knees, she unceremoniously pulled the plug from her body, evoking a chorus of groans from outside the cage.

"No! Put back. Not done yet!"

"Do over! Big finish."

"Not good. Captain not like this. No bid. No bid."

Annie had broken our invented rapport with the crowd. The show was over—and they weren't hesitating to voice their disapproval.

Ignoring the taunts and jeers from the disappointed men, Annie inspected the plug, tilting the base back and forth as she examined it in the dull, gray light.

"The little mark, the symbol, whatever it is, it's really hard to see. The surface has been polished so many times it's worn down the metal." She glanced at my bottom. "Let me look at yours."

The crowd continued heckling us, some of their comments carrying the threat of punishment.

"Bitches need whipping."

"Not trained. Make lower price."

"Get captain. He fix this."

"Try to relax," Annie said. "You're holding on to it. Relax and let go."

I did my best to decompress as she gently pulled the plug from my butt.

Annie stood, turning the metal in her hands. I had no idea what she was looking for. With the exception of the jeweled plug the captain had provided for the pre-auction pictures, the only anal toys I'd seen were made of silicone or plastic.

Grateful for the opportunity to get off my knees, I rose to my feet and stared into the disgruntled crowd. I didn't see the American buyer. He'd either stepped back into the smoke and haze or around to the blind side of the container. Hopefully, he'd overlooked Annie's impulsive decision to suspend our play and was still interested in bidding on us as a pair.

"NO! Oh, God. NO!" Annie's anguished cry echoed off the steel walls.

I turned and saw her hurl both plugs against the back of the cage, the steel projectiles bouncing off the corrugated metal with a loud bang.

"Jewel, the holes in these plugs, they're…" She choked, unable to continue.

I heard it in her voice—the tormenting agony of pure fear. It set off something in the pit of my stomach that I hadn't felt since R.J. had tied me to the floor of the van and strangled me until I was nearly unconscious.

"Annie? What's wrong?"

We were only a few steps apart, but with every second of silence, I felt the separation grow. I was losing her, and I didn't know why.

She closed her eyes and shook her head. Her face etched in pain, her struggle to talk was useless. Before I could get to her, she dropped to her knees and buried her face in her hands, her wretched sobbing as heartbreaking as a death rattle.

I draped my arms around her. "You're scaring me," I scolded. "I don't know what's going on. Talk to me."

Her words came in short bursts, each whispered on a separate gasp of air. "The plugs, they're not toys . . ."

"What?"

The crowd was finally disbursing, their mumbled curses and vulgar remarks a cruel reminder of their self-centered arrogance. Instead of concern over Annie's obvious distress, they expressed only distain and contempt.

I spotted the buyer. He'd retreated to the same position he'd used when R.J. delivered the plugs to us. He was watching, but something about him was different. He seemed fascinated, even spellbound by Annie's outburst. Seeing me notice him, he began walking toward the front of the cage.

With a breaking voice, Annie tried again. "The symbol, the one stamped into the base..." She swallowed hard, fighting to regain control. "It's a plus sign," she managed. "On yours, too."

I shook my head, still not understanding.

"The holes, they're electrical connections… terminals, to wire us up."

I closed my eyes, the patchy black gaps in my vision telling me I was on the verge of passing out. I reached out, searching for the floor, hoping I could prevent myself from hitting my head on the steel plate. In the background, I could hear men talking, some of them grumbling about the quick ending of our performance.

Annie cleared her throat. I sensed her moving, getting to her feet.

Fighting the nausea, I opened my eyes. "Annie, it can't be Gregory. He's not wearing glasses. Remember? You told me he has to wear really thick lenses. This guy doesn't have any trouble seeing, in fact, his eyes are two different colors. It's almost if they—"

"Used to belong to someone else?" She finished my sentence.

"That's not possible. They wouldn't take eyes from two different donors unless . . ."

Annie nodded with a look of sick disgust. "The donors weren't dead."

I wasn't ready to believe it, yet it made horrifying sense. Black-market body parts taken from the living was a thriving business in this part of the world. "Annie, we have to be sure. We can't take anything for granted."

She wasn't listening. She was already heading to the front of the container to meet the American buyer head-on.

She stopped a foot from the wire.

"You never told us your name." There was a slight quiver in her voice, then an increase in volume as she tried to hide it. "Mine's Annie," she added. "What's yours?"

He ignored her question. "I gave you those plugs as presents. I was hoping you'd wear them for a while. Wasn't very nice of you to toss them aside like that. Now I'm not sure if you're worth my time, or my money."

His personality had changed again, to that of an arrogant, flippant little snot. Completely dismissing Annie's breakdown, he didn't care how she felt, even though his "gifts" were the obvious source of her torment.

"I'll bet I know what your name is," Annie continued. "It's Gregory, isn't it?"

He cocked his head, staring at her in the same way he might when looking at an unusual breed of animal, evaluating its strength and stamina.

Tired of him dodging her questions, Annie went for the jugular. "You use electricity, don't you?"

He looked down for a moment, his expression not of shock or stunned disbelief, but of jaded boredom. While I was fairly certain he hadn't expected a confrontation from someone who was naked, pretty, and on the opposite side of the wire, it didn't seem to affect him, either. He raised his head and stared at Annie, his smoldering silence his only answer.

His defiance sent Annie over the edge. She flew against the wire, slamming her fists on the unforgiving knots of twisted steel. "You murdering piece of shit. Go on, deny it. Tell me you're somebody else—somebody who just happens to walk around a slave auction with electrodes in his pocket."

His face began to brighten, his emerging smile suggesting not only an admission of guilt, but a willingness to reveal his true nature.

Annie's hands were shaking, her breathing erratic and forced. "I know who you are," she continued. "There's no point trying to hide it."

Finally, he spoke. "What else do you know?"

Driven by hate and anger, Annie shifted from side-to-side, never breaking her fierce lock on Gregory's Frankensteinian eyes. "You're the insane asshole who killed Eve." She sucked at the stale air, then added, "And you need to die."

Annie was seething, wanting blood. Without the wire to separate them, she would have set on him with a single intent—to kill him.

She'd realized the true purpose of the butt plugs after recognizing the symbols stamped into the base. The plus signs were electrical terminal markings, designating the polarity for direct current. From there, she had quickly drawn the heartbreaking and ironically fatal conclusion that the young American was Gregory Housing, a madman and sadistic predator. Our efforts to entertain him, to convince him to buy us, had been an audition for torture and eventual electrocution.

"Well, you perverted fuck. You going to admit it or not?"

Any doubt over Gregory's true identity vanished as his mismatched eyes fixed on Annie's throat. No longer able to camouflage his true personality, his transformation was as graphic as it was ugly. "Maybe you are worth my time after all," he hissed.

I knew there was more Annie wanted to say, but she was mute with rage. She could only watch as Gregory backed away, his forced show of clenched teeth making it plain he wasn't finished with her.

My near faint had left me with an unsettled stomach. In spite of the nausea, I had to talk Annie down. "He's gone now," I said. "We know who he is and what he looks like. If he comes back, we'll tell everyone within earshot what kind of monster he really is."

I began unhooking Annie's fingers from the wire. The bolt of adrenaline that had turned her muscles into steel cords was exhausted. Limp as a rag doll, she collapsed into my arms.

There wasn't time to console her. Our situation had gone from bad to worse, and we needed a lot more than an impassioned heart-to-heart.

As I lowered her to the floor, she asked the obvious. "What do we do now?"

I cringed at the desperation in her voice, as if we'd been digging a tunnel to freedom and discovered we were ten feet short of the fence.

"We can't let him take us," I whispered. "If he buys us, we'll have to fight, run."

I had no idea how we could win the kind of defensive battle I was suggesting. Neither of us tipped the scale at much over a hundred pounds. And if Gregory was the successful bidder, his hired muscle would be ready in reserve. Our chances of escaping during the transfer of ownership would be next to impossible.

I kept it to myself.

"What the hell did you say to him?" R.J. had run from the front of the building, responding to complaints from auction officials about one of the white girls going ballistic. He looked every bit as frantic as a nine-year-old who'd lost a pocketful of change on the playground.

Annie jumped at the sound of R.J.'s voice. "Not near what he deserved," she screamed. "If I'd had a gun, I would have killed the fucking bastard."

There wasn't much fight left in her, but it was enough to make R.J. wish he'd used a better choice of words.

Several men turned from their conversations to see what had prompted Annie's new outburst. Protesting girls were not unusual at the auction, but their tirades usually consisted of incoherent ranting—easy to ignore. This had been a well-articulated threat directed at a specific buyer, and made by a girl who was in obvious possession of her faculties.

"Jesus, Annie, shut your mouth!" R.J. looked around at the startled men, waving them off in an effort to minimize Annie's vow of vengeance. "You know the rules and what they can do to you for talking like that."

"Better here and now than to let that asshole put his hands on me!"

Annie's defiant behavior had R.J. completely rattled. He turned to me. "Jewel, try to calm her down. I'll find the captain, tell him what's going on."

"You do that," Annie yelled. "You go find the captain. You tell him about that murdering piece of shit Gregory. And don't forget to tell him about how he sold Eve to that fucker, and how Gregory killed her for the sheer pleasure of it." Annie's fading voice reflected her depleting stamina, but the fire in her eyes made it clear she was far from finished. "And remind him that if he sells us to that scum-bag, he's just as guilty. Because he knows what the bastard will do to us."

R.J. looked down at the floor and exhaled in frustration. "I'll be back."

Several men had gathered around the cage, curious over Annie's meltdown. Concerned their interest might set her off again, I nudged her into the back corner, away from the wire.

"Gregory won't want us, not now," I assured her. "He knows we're hard to handle, a real nightmare. That's not what he's looking for. He wants someone naive and complacent, a girl with no idea what he plans to do to her."

For the longest time, Annie remained quiet, her only movement an occasional swipe at a random tear streaking her face.

Finally, she looked out into the crowd. "That fucking parasite should have his throat ripped out." It came out as matter-of-fact, as if she were commenting on the need to remove a stray weed from the garden.

I nodded, not only because I agreed with her, but because I'd already added Gregory's name to *the list*.

R.J. emerged from the crowd. He'd only been gone a few minutes. Either the captain's response had been short and to the point or he was too busy to talk with him. The auction was about to start and he was no doubt swamped with last minute details. Either way, I wanted to shield Annie from his approach, give her a few more seconds of relative peace before we were forced to listen to more whiney-assed complaints about Annie's behavior.

He slowed as he approached the cage. "How's she doing?"

Without speaking, I motioned him to back away, to leave us alone.

He shook his head. "Can't. This is important. I need to talk to you."

"Go away," I said. "We're tired of your bullshit."

R.J. pursed his lips, blowing out an exasperated breath. If we had been anywhere else, he would have yelled at us, threatened us with punishment. But here, in front of potential buyers, we had him on eggshells. Whatever he had to tell us, he would have to do it without creating a disturbance. Any more shouting or signs of belligerence from either side of the cage could have a drastic effect on the bidding.

Annie lifted her head. "Let's find out what the idiot has to say."

As I helped Annie to her feet, I noticed a faint sign of relief on R.J.'s face.

"Over here," he said, then as an afterthought he added, "Please." Apparently, he didn't want our conversation to be overheard.

A foot from the wire, Annie stopped me short. "Close enough." She looked at R.J. "Okay, horse-face, what's so important?"

R.J. hesitated, glancing back at the crowd, then at the floor—everywhere but us.

"Spill it, R.J., or we're going back to our cozy little corner." Annie wasn't cutting him any slack.

"I talked to the captain."

"And?"

"That guy you were yelling at, he talked to the captain, too."

Annie inhaled, ready to launch another verbal attack. I jumped in before she could speak, hoping to keep her calm. "Okay, so you and the asshole kid told the captain how bad we were. So what did 'ol blood and guts say?"

"Yeah, about that." He hesitated long enough to look behind, then to both sides to make sure no one could overhear. "First, Annie has to stop screaming. If she makes any more trouble, the captain wants me to gag her. He's not fucking around. He means it. He told me to get the rest of the men if I needed them."

His discretion—and restraint—in using his favorite form of discipline surprised me. A few hours ago, the prospect of ramming a ball-gag down either of our throats would have had him drooling. But something had diffused his mean streak, and it was apparently more important than his need to hurt us.

It sounded like Annie's threat to kill Gregory had generated complaints, pushing the limits of what auction officials would allow, regardless of the amount of money at stake.

I turned my head toward Annie's ear. "Let's tell him what he wants to hear," I whispered. "We can't let him gag us. We need to be able to talk."

Annie's expression remained hard, unforgiving. But she nodded—once.

I looked at R.J. "Okay, we'll behave. Anything else?"

"That guy...Gregory. He wants Annie tied up, chained to the back of the cage. Otherwise, he said he won't bid."

The breath seized in my chest. Annie leaned against me, to keep from slumping to the floor.

"And?" My voice fell to a near-whisper.

R.J.'s blank stare told me he wasn't following.

"Are you going to do it . . . tie her up?"

R.J. shrugged his shoulders. "The captain told Gregory he'd think about it. Probably wants to pull an offer out of the guy first, to see how much money he's got before he makes up his mind."

The captain's hesitation in chaining Annie to the cage prior to the bidding had nothing to do with the additional discomfort she would be forced to endure. It was simply good business. While securing Annie with handcuffs and rope would make it easier for Gregory to transport her—if he was the successful bidder—doing it beforehand was premature. Assuming *any* buyer had the financial resources to outbid all others was financial conjecture at best, and risky speculation on the part of a seller. More important, other buyers could easily interpret Annie's early binding as confirmation the captain had decided to sell us separately, a move that might reduce the total amount of money he hoped to receive from bidders who had specifically come to buy us as a pair.

Still, Gregory's ultimatum was both unusual and worrisome. Taken at face value, his request to have Annie bound and ready for travel suggested he planned to spend whatever was necessary to outbid other buyers. I wanted to believe it was male bravado, a knee-jerk reaction to Annie's accusations, meant to scare her for verbally attacking him in public.

"R.J., you know Gregory is total bullshit," I said. "He's playing this cat-and-mouse game, trying to get inside Annie's head. It's all part of his twisted personality. He uses men to stroke his ego. He uses women to satisfy his sick, perverted fantasies, and then kills them in the process."

He stared at me with placating indifference.

"Don't you get it?" I asked. "He's fucking crazy!"

Before R.J. could respond, Annie added, "You're acting like you don't know who Gregory is. You're not that stupid, R.J."

"I don't want to know who he is," he said. "The guy's got two bodyguards constantly shadowing him. Either one of them could decide to kick my balls for asking too many questions. And anyway, it's not my business. It's up to the captain now."

Annie shook her head in disgust. "You're no better than Gregory, and just as guilty. I hope someday you're made to pay for it."

R.J. began backing away, afraid Annie was on the verge of another outburst.

"Remember Eve?" she asked, her voice rising.

The question stopped him in his tracks.

"She spent two weeks on the *Kelsey*," Annie reminded him. "And when the captain finally let you fuck her, it was all you talked about for days."

R.J. shuffled from one foot to the other. "Yeah, I kinda remember."

"Kinda? You went on and on about how pretty she was, how innocent she looked. You even said if you had the money, you would buy her yourself."

His forehead gathered in heavy furrows.

"You wanna know what she told me?"

R.J. shrugged.

"She believed you when you told her you would watch out for her, protect her." She paused, her voice about to break. "She trusted you."

"She told you that?"

"She told me everything. Right up until the captain sold her to Gregory. Then she couldn't tell anybody anything. Because when the bastard was done with her, she was dead. He tied her to a table and turned up the voltage until her heart burst." She swallowed hard, struggling to stay in control. "Jesus, R.J., doesn't that mean anything to you?"

R.J.'s twisted mouth reflected the strain of hearing the truth. Maybe he realized in some ways, he and Gregory had a lot more in common than he wanted to admit.

He lifted both hands, palms up. "I don't know what to tell you, Annie. I'm just doing my job."

I'd only seen the look of fear on R.J. once before, in the life raft after the *Kelsey* went down, as he desperately worked to keep us from capsizing in the storm. Now he faced a different kind of threat. Their conversation was beginning to attract attention, and if Annie did explode with another angry lecture, *he* would be seen as the source of agitation—and would have to pay the consequences.

"I'm just doing my job," he repeated. He took another step backward before turning and quickly walking out of sight.

"Annie?" It took a moment for her to realize I was speaking. Turning to face me, I saw her bottom lip was bleeding, split from the pressure of her own bite. She shook her head in surrender, the tears spilling from her eyes.

Her memories of Eve were heartbreaking. But I knew it was more than that. Her mind had moved forward into her own horrific future—strapped to the killing table, her openings filled with electrodes, her terrified screams unable to penetrate the soundproofed walls. And Gregory standing next to her, his hands hovering over her naked body, savoring the tiny blue arcs of corona radiating from her quivering skin, hoping he could prolong the time, extend his pleasure for as long as possible before the current finally drove Annie's heart into cardiac arrest.

Chapter Nineteen

The bidding process was unlike any auction I'd ever seen—with one exception. The sale of each girl began with a "barker" walking across the elevated selling platform while holding a large white-board displaying the lot number. A corresponding number, taped over the top of each occupied cage, provided buyers with a confirming reference of which girl was being offered for sale.

But that's where the similarity ended. Instead of a fast-talking auctioneer asking for bids from the crowd, sellers sat behind a line of folding tables, collecting written bids submitted on small squares of paper. Indicating the current highest bid by pressing an index finger to the appropriate paper square, the seller then called out the amount, sweeping the other bids to the floor.

Although the number of times a buyer could bid was entirely optional, all sellers were required to complete the transaction in three minutes. When an owner was certain he'd obtained the maximum price buyers were willing to pay, he would declare the girl sold, accept payment, and transfer any "boot"—the girl's clothes, shoes, or other personal possessions—to the new owner.

I wondered if there was a notary to give the proceeding an air of official sanction—if Annie and I would come with some kind of title, with all the blanks filled in, confirming the year of manufacture and mileage.

"When they brought you in, did you see the number on the top of our cage?" Annie was standing against the wire, looking up, straining to see the piece of torn notebook paper taped to the steel frame. It had been intentionally placed out of reach.

"I don't remember. It didn't register."

Annie waved at one of the passing men, a standout because of his suit and tie. "Hey, tiger, what's our number?"

The man raised his hands in the international gesture for not speaking the language.

"The number, silly. You don't need English to hold up your fingers." Annie brought her hands to her breasts and squeezed.

In seconds, he was standing in front of her, a huge smile across his face.

"Up there." She pointed to the top of the container. "Grab that piece of paper for me.

Let me see it." Annie tried to convey her request with sign language, reaching up then lowering her hand, as if pulling down a window shade.

"You know he can't do that." R.J. walked up from the side, the angle keeping us from seeing his approach. "And he knows it, too. If he pulled that number down, security would be all over his ass."

"Then tell us. It won't make any difference. At least not to you."

"Might make a big difference, especially if you get all crazy and start yelling when your turn comes up. I could get my ass kicked."

Annie centered him in her sights. "You're a fucking wuss. You *deserve* to have your ass kicked."

He shook his head in condescending dismissal. "I always said you had the biggest balls of anybody on the boat. I'm gonna miss you, Annie."

"Too bad you feel that way," Annie sighed. "You could have had both of us, me and Jewel, right here and now. Would have been one hell of a party, too." She paused, then added, "But we're reserved for men, not little boys."

She was baiting him. Maybe I could help. I stepped beside her. "You remember what it was like, don't you? That last night on the *Kelsey*, when you took your turn fucking both of us?"

I didn't expect much of a reaction. R.J. was a sadist to the core, his pleasure kindled by the pain of others. I was surprised to see his eyes glazing, his breathing turning rapid and shallow.

"I remember," he said.

"So just tell us what number we drew," I said. "We want to know how much longer we have to wait. Then you can come inside the cage and play with us for as long as you want, to help pass the time."

"We promise we won't tell anyone," Annie added. "Then you can have us one more time, you know, something to remember us by."

We were relentless, determined to break him down.

"My goodness, you girls are a real enterprising pair. If I didn't know better, I'd swear you were attempting to persuade this young man to do something against his better judgment. And at the moment, with all that blood redirected to other parts of his anatomy, it's apparent you definitely have the advantage."

The man's southern drawl was as pronounced as his neatly-styled white hair and precisely trimmed beard. And yet, each word rang clear and distinct, his deep, solid voice polishing each syllable with eloquent perfection. Patently American, his rotund stature gave him the appearance of a jovial grandfather in his mid-sixties. With his genial, nonthreatening manner and a slightly mischievous smile, he was immediately disarming—and conspicuously out of place. I wondered if he'd taken a wrong turn while scouting new locations for a chicken franchise.

It sounded like he'd heard most if not all of our conversation, listening from the side of the container, outside our line of sight. His sudden appearance pulled R.J. back from the edge of surrender.

"They're both American," R.J. stammered. "And they aren't shy about getting with each other. Pretty smart, too." It was a quick sales pitch, but his bright red face was a dead giveaway as he tried to recover from nearly being sucker-fucked.

"I can see their obvious attributes, but tell me son, what on earth are they doing here? Pretty young things, all trussed up in a cage?"

"Well, sir, they were brought in by the captain, and if you'd like, I can make arrangements for you to speak with him about their—"

"Why don't you leave us a spell?" the older gentleman interrupted. "Give us a chance to become better acquainted."

R.J. nearly bowed, his need to defer to the white-haired senior seemingly done as much out of fear as respect. He retreated a good twenty feet.

"Well, ladies, now that the young man has taken his leave, we find ourselves with the opportunity to talk, but only if it pleases you as much as it would favor me."

For the first time since arriving at the auction, I felt the embarrassment of being naked and on display. This outwardly friendly stranger was addressing us as equals, and it made our predicament—the insanity, the degradation—all the more obvious. I moved next to Annie. The additional privacy was only imagined, but I felt a bit less exposed.

"What do you want to talk about?" Annie asked, her voice dripping with suspicion. First impressions meant nothing here, and while this stranger projected the persona of a polite, southern gentleman, his mere presence at a slave auction tarnished his credibility. Somewhere beneath all that gracious and well-mannered civility, he harbored a self-serving agenda. And until we knew more about him, giving him the benefit of the doubt was out of the question.

He smiled, revealing perfect, white teeth. "My name is Robert, although the ladies I employ often call me Bobby. I answer to both."

I'd not seen him before, either from a distance or in the crowd of men who had stood outside the wire and blatantly gawked at our pussies and tits. No, from his stance and sheer presence, I would remember.

"I won't bore you with the obvious," he continued. "But before I cut to the chase, I want you to know how sympathetic I am to your situation. I've heard the stories, about how you girls wind up in these terrible auctions. And how the street pimps and flesh brokers take advantage of runaways and destitute young women, turning them into working girls. It's a sad state of affairs, no question. But you two still have that freshness about you, as if you came looking for a party and ended up with the wrong crowd." His eyes never strayed from our faces.

"We're not party girls," I said softly.

Bobby's expression turned pensive. "How you got here is not as important as how you find your way out. Especially when you consider a few of these men have some very unusual ideas about how they plan to use the women they buy. Many of them treat their charges with no more compassion than they would a lame horse."

Since my reunion with Annie, I had tried to be the strong one. But now, I couldn't stop the tears. This man, who looked like he'd stepped out of a stately Southern mansion, was painting a picture of our future with bleak shades of desperation and despair. I knew we were in trouble, and throwing the details in my face wasn't helping.

I felt Annie's arm sliding around my shoulder, offering comfort as best she could.

"Now, now, I didn't mean to upset you," Bobby added. "But I thought it was important you know how serious your situation really is."

"We know," I managed. "There's a lunatic out there who wants to pump a couple hundred volts up our ass so he can listen to us scream."

Bobby's forehead buckled into furrowed rows. "You wouldn't by chance be talking about a young man who goes by the name of Gregory?"

"The same," Annie said.

He brought his fingers to his chin, his expression turning thoughtful. "Someday, the authorities are gonna find that boy with a bullet in his head. And as much as it pains me to say it, the world will be better off for the loss."

More than his condemnation of Gregory, I saw his face expressing concern. Perhaps it was the intended result of a well-practiced routine, but his interest in our welfare seemed sincere. Although I had no idea what his motives were, he reminded me of a grandparent who preferred second chances over punishment.

He took a deep, exaggerated breath and blew it out, as if expelling the lingering image of Gregory from the conversation. "I'll get to the point," he said. "I'm what you would call a *recruiter*. I scout the nightclubs, bars, and the occasional auction, looking for intelligent young women who have the desire to escape their situation. And if I'm convinced of their intentions, of their desire to work toward the eventual end of their inscription, I offer them an opportunity to serve a useful cause." He paused. "Perhaps even a necessary one."

The drawl and accent were still there, but Bobby's rhetoric confirmed he was no country bumpkin. He was an articulate negotiator, his exacting choice of words making his story all the more believable.

In the background, amplified announcements began echoing through the building.

The auction was starting.

Most of the men broke off their conversations and started moving toward the bidding platform. A few walked back and forth between the cages, revisiting their favorites, reconsidering their choices as they decided on a final selection.

"What does that have to do with us?" Annie asked. "Give us the bottom line."

Bobby responded with a single nod, his quick wink and a momentary flash of teeth meant to be reassuring. "Yes, time is short, so I'll be quick. My employer is an off-the-books department of the government. It's my job to procure young ladies who have the necessary qualifications to act as *hostesses.*"

I started at him with impatient confusion. "Hostesses?"

Annie was more to the point. "I'm sure you're talking about something other than serving cookies at a Friday night social. What would we *really* be doing?"

"There can be some variations in the assignment, but your primary responsibility would be to entertain visiting dignitaries and important business associates, for specialized government interests."

The announcements continued to boom over the loudspeaker, the bidding instructions being repeated in French and Thai.

"Which government?" Annie injected.

Her question surprised me as much as it did Bobby. "Why, yours and mine," he answered. "The only one that counts."

"Bullshit," Annie challenged. "There's no such thing as government prostitutes."

"Hostesses," Bobby countered. He paused, then added, "You may be surprised to learn that in some situations, our young women can be every bit as important as having troops on the ground. In fact, there are many instances in which the activities of our ladies have prevented violent conflict, saving lives in the process."

Numba wan! Numba wan! The auctioneer was calling the first bid number.

Excitement rippled through the building. In the distance, I could see buyers pressing toward the tables. I imagined the seller of the first lot readying himself to receive and negotiate the bids.

"Bobby, what's the number on the top of our cage?" I wanted to know how much time we had. I wasn't sure what this guy was offering—if anything. But if there was an alternative to taking our chances with Gregory or one of the seedy-looking men gathered at the front of the building, I wanted to hear it.

He responded with an exaggerated look of regret. "In spite of how much I would like to tell you, I'm sure you understand my predicament. If I reveal anything about the auction process that would be deemed a violation of the rules, I could be subjected to severe consequences, the least of which would be to bar me from attending future auctions. He paused for a moment, his roguish grin breaking through. "So please interpret my willingness to put myself at risk as an indication of my sincere intent." He dropped his voice to a whisper and leaned in. "You're lot number five. I would estimate about fifteen minutes before you're offered for sale."

Fifteen minutes. I didn't know whcthcr to bc relieved or terrified. In light of Bobby's conversation, the number meant nothing. He needed to reveal something useful.

"So, you're offering us a job?" I asked.

"Actually, much more than that." Bobby paused, creating a bit of eager anticipation. "It's a career position within our government's most clandestine department."

Before I could speak, Annie asked the question we were both thinking. "Dress it up any way you like, but you're still talking about us having sex with strangers, right?" It was a challenge, essentially calling Bobby a purveyor of half-truths, his rhetoric an attempt to cloak the less respectable aspects of international politics in a blur of flag-waving mumbo-jumbo.

Bobby answered without hesitation. "Yes, sex can be one of the more useful tools, to relax the mind and loosen the tongue. It's especially helpful when gathering intelligence. Done correctly, it's an art form, providing

261

companionship in exchange for trust, convincing the suspicious they are among friends. And in my opinion, our girls do it better, and with more finesse, than anyone else in the world."

Numba tu! Numba tu! The speaker system blared out confirmation of the first sale and the start of the second. The bidding was moving quickly.

"You mean, we'd work like a spy?" I couldn't think of another way of describing what Bobby was suggesting. Not that it made his proposal sound more agreeable, but it gave him the opportunity to deny it, to pull back the pretty wrapping and tell us the truth.

"Your official designation would be *international relations specialist*, with an appropriate government service rating for purposes of compensation."

"We would live here?" Annie asked. "In Bangkok?"

"Initially. There's a training period to increase your knowledge of international customs and practices. Then you'll be sent to where the need is most urgent. To answer your question, many of the girls live in embassy housing."

"So you're saying we could wind up anywhere?"

Bobby seemed to know what I was really asking. "No, dear. Our domestic operations are completely separate. Your assignment would be international . . . Europe, Asia, even South America."

I felt like we were conducting an inquisition, but Bobby didn't seem to mind, and I wanted as much information as possible. "For how long?"

"A five-year contract is required. Upon its conclusion, you will receive the appropriate severance benefit and if you choose, an offer of more conventional employment."

Announcements blared from the loudspeakers. The second girl had been sold.

As far as I was concerned, there was nothing to think about. Even if Bobby's offer was only half true, it sounded less dangerous than trying to escape from an abusive owner and hiding in dark alleys while working our way back to the States. Although we would still be in the sex business—no doubt required to do things we would find unpleasant—his proposal was more than the assurance of a roof over our head and three meals a day. It was the promise of a future, of getting out alive, with the opportunity to start life over.

I looked at Annie. She nodded.

"Okay, what do we have to do?" I expected Bobby to pull out a contract or some other paperwork to confirm our agreement.

"You tell me you're ready to go and we can move forward. But first, I need you to understand something." Bobby's eyes narrowed, his voice losing its playful inflection. "Once you agree, there's no going back, no changing your minds. Obedience to your superiors is absolutely mandatory. You can't question anything from here on out. You've got a real chance to turn yourselves around, and if you're smart and do a good job, there's no telling where you might end up."

Numba tree! Numba tree! The voice over the loudspeaker swept through the building like a harbinger of fate. We were running out of time.

Our options were simple: We could agree to Bobby's offer or take our chances with another buyer—*one of which could be Gregory*.

Annie answered first. "I'm good with that."

"You too, Jewel?" Bobby looked at me as if he could see deep into my brain, searching

264

my memories, evaluating my thoughts. I wondered how he knew my name.

"Yes, count me in."

"And one last thing," he added. "I don't use handcuffs or any type of restraint. If you do this, you do it of your own free will. You'll be expected to honor your part of the bargain throughout the term of your contract. But if you run, if you try to leave, we won't want you back. The department has a saying: *Once a runner, always a runner.* And we use the same people to track and retrieve runaways as most of the traders in this building, so don't entertain the idea I'm offering you a reprieve that will later give you a chance to escape.

Although, under the circumstances, it was a minor point, there was something about his logic that didn't make sense. "I don't understand," I said. "If you don't want runners back, why pay a bounty-hunter to find them?"

Bobby looked at me the way my father did the night he told me my dog had been run over. "To tie up any loose ends."

I felt Annie squeeze my arm. She understood. So did I. This man's offer was drastically different than what we could expect from any other man in this building. Bobby and the people he worked for, saw no advantage in using the stinging end of a whip as a method of control. Their priorities were based on keeping the machinery of state running smoothly. Exceptions would not be tolerated. Bobby was telling us flat out, without reservation, if we fucked up there would be fatal consequences. It meant forgetting about the idea of escape and, instead, making a total commitment to new jobs as high-class hookers.

I was sure there was a lot more Bobby wasn't telling us, but I hoped his omissions were minor and incidental, and not the intentional withholding of critical information that would make us regret ever having met him.

I wondered . . . in five years, would we look back on our decision to trust this amenable gentleman with a prominent southern drawl as shrewd and insightful, or just another detour in a life punctuated by a hijacked youth and a kidnapped future?

I spoke quickly. "We're ready."

Bobby smiled, his entire demeanor suggesting he would have opened his arms in a welcoming hug if the wire had not prevented it. "I'll make a phone call. Have to leave the building to do it. You sit tight, and I'll see what I can do about getting you some clothes."

Annie sighed. "We'll wait for you right here. We promise."

Bobby chuckled as he walked away. It sounded spontaneous, but I knew it was for our benefit—to leave us with a sense of assurance.

"Jewel? You think we did the right thing?"

It wasn't doubt I saw on Annie's face as much as exhaustion.

"We've never been offered the *right* thing," I said. "But right now, we don't have a choice. We have to go along with this guy. It makes more sense, safer." I paused, realizing my reasoning was based on an extremely important assumption—that Bobby had told us the truth. "And besides," I added, "he didn't say for sure, but maybe they'll let us share living quarters, work together as a team."

Her face brightened. "As long as we can take the first month to sleep."

Chapter Twenty

Numba fo! Numba fo!

I looked toward the bidding platform. The harsh glare from the skylights cut the haze with extreme contrast, washing the entire scene in grainy shadow. It resembled an old black-and-white movie, with a crowd of unrecognizable men shuffling in front of the elevated tables and, between them, the occasional glimpse of a slight man walking back and forth, brandishing his white-board.

I reached for Annie's hand. "We're next. It won't be much longer."

She laid her head on my shoulder and closed her eyes. Her fear and anger were subsiding. Without a full charge of adrenalin pumping through her veins, she was ready to collapse.

There was nothing left to do but wait. No doubt Bobby wielded a formidable level of authority, but he was still an employee. I imagined his boss to be a faceless, even nameless superior who knew his subordinates only by the tone and tenor of their speech—probably confirmed by voice recognition software. Hopefully, the sensitive nature of this part of the business allowed them to circumvent the bureaucratic red tape associated with the majority of government purchases.

I began to think about my new job, what it would be like, with its presumably affluent surroundings and appurtenant civility. Oh, I knew the men would be the same, their perpetual need to fuck a pretty girl always first and foremost on their minds. But perhaps they would practice the courtesy of asking first, allowing both of us to pretend I actually had a choice in the matter.

If Bobby's description of our new jobs was accurate, it sounded like Annie and I would be playing the part of friend, lover, and confidant. Like chameleon actors, we would transform ourselves into the ideal woman for the assigned mark. With our interests quickly aligning with his, we would exhibit obvious fascination for his superior intelligence and quick wit. And if he turned out to be one of those rare men with little to say, it would be our job to encourage some pillow talk. Even if meaningless to us, an innocent disclosure could be the last and vital piece of information in a scheme of international chicanery.

It sounded like a premise drawn from the pages of an Ian Fleming novel. But my decision to serve the designs of freedom and democracy with the total surrender of my body wasn't motivated by the thrill of living in the high-stakes world of espionage. Bobby's offer had struck at the core of my basic instinct to survive—I wanted out of this nightmare, and I wanted out *now*.

Numba fi! Numba fi!

Our turn.

I tried to guess how much Bobby would have to pay for us. Two hundred thousand, at least. And from what I knew about the value of two attractive, drug-free white girls, that amount could be low. The economics were the same as in any business—price was based on supply and demand. While the number of pimps who had that kind of money was few, those who could afford it knew their wealthiest customers would easily pay ten thousand dollars to be the first to fuck us, just for bragging rights.

I guided Annie to the back of the cage. Sitting on the steel floor, we couldn't see the activity surrounding the bidding tables. But it was easy to imagine the captain sorting through the slips of paper, reviewing the numbers, then looking up at each bidder, trying to determine if a buyer was pledging every last dime of his available cash.

As far as I was concerned, the captain's *real* payday was still in the future, when I, or someone I had paid, would deliver his notice of retirement—his just and final compensation for dealing in skin.

Numba sis! Numba sis!

It was over.

And fast. Apparently you can't outbid Uncle Sam.

I stroked the back of Annie's head. "It's done. Bobby will be here soon. You think the captain will hand us over in the parking lot?"

"That's how it worked in Yangon. Not sure how it's done here." She had pushed herself to answer. Exhaustion was shutting her down.

"He's probably too busy counting his money," I said. "But if the captain does show up, I'm going to say goodbye with a swift kick to his balls."

She smiled. Her eyes were drooping, her head bobbing slightly. With our safety assured, she was finally allowing herself the gift of sleep.

I scooted to the side, laying her head in my lap, wishing I could make her more comfortable.

A half hour passed. Annie drifted in and out, her slumber broken by the blaring speaker system, the voices of passing men, and the sound of heavy traffic in the distance.

My butt was killing me. I had to move. Carefully placing Annie's arm beneath her head, I slipped out from under her.

Standing by the wire, I waited for Bobby to emerge from the ashen gray shroud of cigarette smoke hanging over the bidding platform. From the vantage point of our cage, the crowd of buyers appeared to be a swarm of shape-shifting specters, their features camouflaged by the haze and glare.

I looked back at Annie. Her small body was tucked in a semi-fetal position, reminding me of images from relief organizations depicting an innocent child lying in the filthy squalor of third world poverty.

At times, I'd actually found a bit of respite inside this foul shipping container, knowing it was the only thing keeping the animals at a safe distance. But now, I was counting the minutes until we could leave this deplorable metal box. Annie and I were on our way to start a new life, and although we would have to resign ourselves to meeting the expectations of our new employer, the word *slave* would not be part of our job title.

I needed to pee. An hour ago, I wouldn't have given a second thought to positioning myself over one of the drainage holes in the floor. But I was better than that now. I had a future, where young women acted with discretion and propriety. I would wait, holding it until I could use a bathroom.

"Jewel?"

My head was down. I hadn't been paying attention.

"Are you ready?" Bobby was approaching the cage, looking hurried, anxious to leave.

"Yes, more than ready. I'll wake Annie."

I turned to retrieve her from the floor, but she'd heard Bobby's voice and was already rising to her feet. I reached for her, smiling. "It's time to go."

Bobby walked past the front of the container and disappeared around the side, toward the door.

"What about clothes?" I asked.

His voice bounced off the steel, hollow and slightly muffled. "I'd hoped to find a more substantial wardrobe, but I'm afraid there wasn't much to choose from. I managed to find a light overcoat. It should do nicely."

The grating bark of the sliding hasp was followed by the raspy squeak of the hinges. The door moved enough for Bobby's face to appear in the opening.

"Here, Jewel, try this on. It's long enough to cover you and will do the trick until we can get something in your size."

I took the tan coat by the collar, noticing the London Fog label. I held it up and turned toward Annie, motioning for her to slip her arms through the sleeves.

"No, Jewel, that one's for you."

"What difference does it make? We're about the same size."

His voice was immediately stern. "Put it on, Jewel. And don't argue with me."

I hesitated, confused with the change in his demeanor. A few minutes ago, he'd been a kind and sympathetic confidante, showing sincere concern over our future. Now that underlying sense of compassion was clearly absent.

"Don't worry about it," Annie assured me. "He just wants to get us out of here without drawing a lot of attention. The hood on that coat will hide your blonde hair. He's probably got something different for me." She grinned. "This is spy stuff, remember?"

The caterwauling door swung wide enough for Bobby to enter, then shut behind him. I didn't think much about it—the impossibility of the door closing on its own.

As I pulled the coat over my shoulders, I noticed he wasn't carrying any other clothing.

"What's Annie going to wear?"

"In a minute." Bobby's voice was terse, his manner abrupt.

I instinctively backed away, pulling Annie with me. Something had changed.

"Look," he began. "This isn't going to be easy, but sometimes it's just the way these things go down." He brought his hands up in a gesture of denied responsibility. "There's a limit to how much I can spend. I knew the bidding would go high, but I never thought—"

"Wait a minute," I interrupted. I felt my stomach begin to churn as Annie tightened her grip on my hand. "What are you saying?"

"I was authorized to spend up to two hundred and fifty thousand. I was sure it would be enough. It wasn't. I was outbid."

Bobby glanced down at the filthy floor, side-stepping the running puddle of my urine as it came within inches of his shoes.

Annie's voice was barely more than a whisper. "He didn't buy both of us."

"Is she right?" My voice was quaking. "You didn't buy us both?"

"I know you wanted to stay together, but the seller had some very strong bids for Annie. As the prices continued to rise, I could only buy one of you." He looked directly into my face. "You, Jewel."

His words hit me like a sudden blow to the head. I stood there, my lower jaw quivering, unable to speak.

I felt Annie sliding to the floor. I couldn't hold her up.

"Who?" she managed. "Who bought me?"

Ignoring her question, Bobby stepped closer. "It's time to go, Jewel." He reached for my arm, the pressure of his grip penetrating the London Fog.

Clutching my free hand, Annie looked up at me, her eyes swelling with fear and panic as the tears began to spill down her cheeks.

"NO!" I shouted. "You promised you would take both of us."

The sting of a syringe broke through my stunned senses. Bobby had pushed the needle though the fabric and into my shoulder. "This will help you relax."

"I won't leave her," I screamed. "That wasn't our deal!"

"The sedative will take effect in a few seconds, then we'll be on our way." Bobby threw the empty syringe into the corner and grabbed me around the waist.

The floor begins to blur. More noise—squawking hinges. Someone is entering the cage.

He's moving toward Annie.

I hear a scream. I can't tell if it came from me or Annie. I feel her fingers desperately holding on to me—and Bobby working to pry them loose.

"Get away from me!" This time I'm sure. It's Annie's voice.

The other man is grabbing her, helping Bobby to drag us apart.

The drugs are shutting down my senses, slowing my reactions.

I'm stumbling, fighting to stay conscious. I trip and nearly fall, feeling the unforgiving resistance of concrete.

I'm outside the cage.

The squealing hinges, the metallic drag of the bolt . . . they're locking the door—with Annie still inside.

Her voice is everywhere, calling to me, yet just outside my reach. I want to hold her, comfort her, tell her I will not give up until—

A man is standing in front of me, blocking my way. I hear Bobby's voice, pushing him back. "This one's mine. The other one's in the cage."

The man nods, the details of his face lost in a slow-motion blur. I try to focus, staring at him through the thickening veil of valium.

Words fall from his mouth. "Won't be near as much fun without you, my little pretty."

He touches my chin, but the feel of his fingers comes moments after I see his hand draw away from my face.

My legs buckle, the first belch of air expanding my cheeks. My stomach empties its contents.

"You gave her too much. Half a syringe would've done it. Now I'll have to carry her." Another voice, from behind me—unfamiliar.

Bobby is talking to someone, telling him to be careful, to watch my head. I feel the dull ache of impact against my shoulder—it's an after-thought, an echo, only part of the pain coming through.

The man who touched me, the one who confessed how my absence would diminish his fun . . . he's sliding the bolt on the cage door, opening it. A thick leather strap trails from his hands like a writhing snake. A coil of rope rides on his shoulder.

A turn of his head releases a glint of light from his left ear. It pierces my eyes like a searing hot flare—the sparkle from a single diamond stud, placed as a finishing touch to a two-hundred-dollar haircut.

Drugged or sober, I know him as well as I know the fear that rakes at my pounding heart.

I try to scream his name, hoping God will hear me, and in His mercy, strike the bastard dead. But I cannot form the words. And instead of Annie consuming my last conscious thoughts, he takes those, too.

The scum of a man who deserved a bullet in the back of his head had made good on his threat—he had come for Annie.

The story continues in Redemption–Book Three – **RedemptionBookThree.com**

Next in the Series
Redemption
Book Three - World Without Love

Rescued from Bangkok's evil flesh markets, Jewel's victory over her captors is bittersweet. Haunted by her last memories of Annie, Jewel vows to do whatever it takes to find her friend—hopefully in time to save her from a sadistic killer. Using her new position as an embassy hostess, Jewel begins to form alliances with the constant stream of visiting political attaches and power brokers, hoping one of them can help find Annie—still alive.

Quick to recognize Jewel's special assets, her supervisors offer her more responsibility, and with it, the benefits of unsupervised travel and the latitude to call her own shots in the completion of her duties. No longer under the scrutiny of the all-seeing covert government network, Jewel realizes she has been given another special privilege, one her superiors could not have anticipated—the freedom to extract revenge on all those who attempted to destroy her life.

But again, the hand fate touches Jewel's heart. And before she can stop herself, a professional relationship becomes very personal, forcing her to choose between the man she loves and the one who helped her escape a dismal world of enslavement and cruel domination.

RedemptionBookThree.com

About the Author

Jaye Frances is the author of seven books including *The New Girl in Town* and the suspense thriller trilogy, *World Without Love*. Her other published works include *The Beach*, *The Kure*, and *Love Travels Forever*. Storyteller, truth-seeker, and optimist, Jaye explores relationships, philosophy, and the complexities of life—a day at a time.

For more info, visit:

JayeFrances.com
JayeFrancesBooks.com
JayeFrancesYouTube.com
JayeFrances.Substack.com
LinkedIn.com/in/JayeFrances
Facebook.com/JayeFrancesAuthor
Twitter.com/JayeFrancesNews

Books by Jaye Frances
World Without Love Series

Betrayed
Book One - World Without Love

Reunion
Book Two - World Without Love

Redemption
Book Three - World Without Love

The New Girl in Town
And Other Journeys Above and Below the Belt

The Beach
Including the Novella, Short Time

The Kure

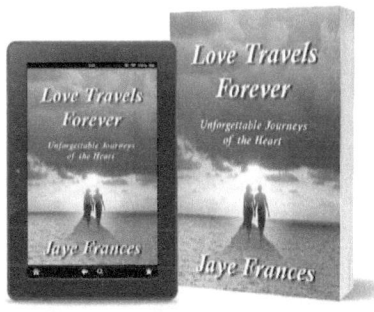

Love Travels Forever

Jaye Frances Books are Available in eBook and Paperback at JayeFrancesBooks.com

World Without Love - The Series
Betrayed – Reunion - Redemption
Betrayed
Book One - *World Without Love*

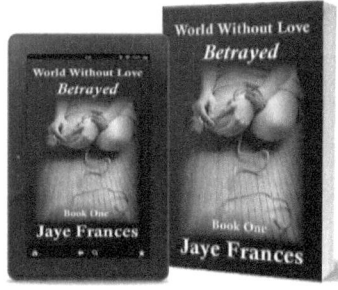

Jewel has everything going for her—a handsome husband, a promising future, and lots of time to explore an island paradise she now calls home. But when a group of strangers accompanies her husband home for a friendly game of poker, her life quickly becomes a hellish nightmare of deceit and betrayal.

Now her very survival depends on entering a world where sex, domination, and money are inseparable, where women must obey all masters, and where every desire has its price.

World Without Love contains mature content and is intended for an 18+ audience

Betrayed is available in eBook and paperback at
BetrayedBookOne.com

Reunion
Book Two - *World Without Love*

In *Reunion*, Jewel's story continues as she finds herself stranded in a far-flung corner of the world. Struggling to elude her captors and a network of bounty hunters, she meets her would-be savior, a man who promises to provide protection and comfort. Believing her nightmare has finally come to an end, Jewel begins making plans to return home, where she can start her life over again.

But greed raises its ugly head, and the terrifying future she thought she'd evaded becomes a reality. Deceived by the only one she believed she could trust, Jewel is left defenseless against the sadistic abusers who take pleasure in teaching her their own form of discipline. With the dream of rescue and returning home to San Diego even further from her reach, she begins planning her revenge on the men who have stolen her life—and her future.

World Without Love contains mature content
and is intended for an 18+ audience

Reunion is available eBook and paperback at
ReunionBookTwo.com

Redemption
Book Three - *World Without Love*

Rescued from Bangkok's evil flesh markets, Jewel's victory over her captors is bittersweet. Haunted by her last memories of Annie, Jewel vows to do whatever it takes to find her friend—hopefully in time to save her from a sadistic killer. Using her new position as an embassy hostess, Jewel begins to form alliances with the constant stream of visiting political attaches and power brokers, hoping one of them can help find Annie—still alive.

Quick to recognize Jewel's special assets, her supervisors offer her more responsibility, and with it, the benefits of unsupervised travel and the latitude to call her own shots in the completion of her duties. No longer under the scrutiny of the all-seeing covert government network, Jewel realizes she has·been given another special privilege, one that her superiors could not have anticipated—the freedom to extract revenge on all those who attempted to destroy her life.

But again, the hand fate touches Jewel's heart. And before she can stop herself, a professional relationship becomes very personal, forcing her to choose between the man she loves and the one who helped her escape a dismal world of enslavement and cruel domination.

World Without Love contains mature content
and is intended for an 18+ audience

Redemption is available in eBook and paperback at
RedemptionBookThree.com

World Without Love – **The Complete Series**
Includes *Betrayed, Reunion, and Redemption*

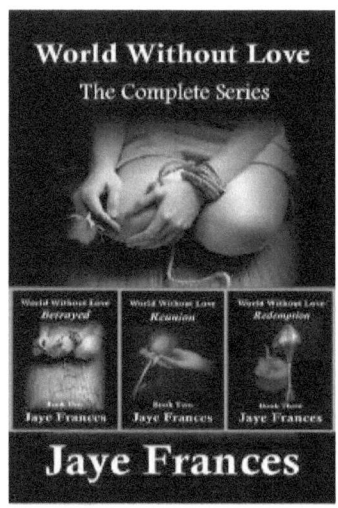

In *Betrayed*, Jewel has everything going for her—a handsome husband, a promising future, and lots of time to explore an island paradise she now calls home. But when a group of strangers accompanies her husband home for a friendly game of poker, her life quickly becomes a hellish nightmare of deceit and betrayal. Now her very survival depends on entering a world where sex, domination, and money are inseparable, where women must obey all masters, and where every desire has its price.

Jewel's story continues in *Reunion*, as she finds herself alone and stranded in a far-flung corner of the world. Struggling to elude her captors and the network of bounty hunters, she meets her would be savior, a man who promises to provide protection and comfort. Jewel believes her nightmare has finally come to an end. But greed raises its ugly head, and the terrifying future she thought she'd evaded becomes a reality—one that seems impossible to escape.

In the final chapter, *Redemption*, Jewel is rescued from Bangkok's evil flesh markets by a covert government agency. Haunted by her last memories of Annie, Jewel vows to do whatever it takes to find her friend—hopefully in time to save her from Gregory's sadistic and murderous intentions. In her new position as an embassy hostess, Jewel forms alliances with political attaches and power brokers, hoping one of them can help her find Annie—still alive.

World Without Love contains mature content
and is intended for an 18+ audience

World Without Love–**The Complete Series** is available
in eBook at **WorldWithoutLove.com**

The New Girl in Town
And Other Journeys Above and Below the Belt

This special collection contains nine of Jaye's most heart-wrenching, mind-tingling, titillating, and thought-provoking stories. Here's a glimpse of what's inside …

- **Our Girl** – Every town has one, and there's always one guy who wants her for his own
- **Three Conversations** – Hindsight often brings wisdom, self-discovery, and a sense of closure—unless the heartache is too much to bear.

- **My First Girlfriend** – There's nothing like a first experience, especially when it brings respect, admiration, and unconditional surrender.

- **The Family Business** – Like mother, like daughter. Until the situation creates a dangerous legacy – and things have to change.

- **The Sighting** – Coming face-to-face with an urban myth can be exciting – and frightening. But when the truth reveals a surprise no one saw coming, it's time for a whole new perspective.

- **Avocados and Fruit Salad** – New beginnings are all around us, if we're willing to recognize the opportunities and take a few risks

- **Younger by Ten** – When love is about the numbers, a few hearts are bound to be broken, especially when you realize your choice of lover had nothing to do with you.

- **A Lie I Desperately Want to Believe** – Trust is often part of the collateral damage when the unquestioning bond of marriage is ripped to shreds.

- **The New Girl in Town** – Sometimes it takes a while to figure out what you want – and build the confidence to go for it!

The New Girl in Town is available in eBook and paperback at **TheNewGirlBook.com**

The Beach

Alan loves the beach. More than a weekend respite, it is his home, his refuge, his sanctuary. And for most of the year, he strolls the sand in blissful solitude, letting nature—and no one else—touch him. But spring has given way to summer, and soon, the annual invasion of vacationers and tourists will subdivide the beach with blankets, umbrellas, and chairs, depriving Alan of his privacy and seclusion—the fundamental touchstones of his life.

Resigned to endure another seasonal onslaught of beach-goers, Alan believes there is nothing he can do but prepare for the worst.

But fate has other plans.

Delivered to him on the crest of a rogue wave, the strange object appears to have no purpose, no practical use—until Alan accidentally discovers what waits inside. Now he must attempt to unravel an ageless mystery, unaware that the final outcome will change his life, and the beach, forever.

In the companion novella *Short Time,* you'll meet a respectable but bored middle-class executive, who exchanges his future for six months of excess and extravagance, only to discover out the price he must pay for his hedonistic indulgence is beyond anything he could have imagined.

The Beach is available in eBook and paperback
at **BewareTheBeach.com**

The Kure

John Tyler, a young man in his early twenties, awakens to find a ghastly affliction taking over his body. When the village doctor offers the conventional, and potentially disfiguring, treatment as the only cure, John tenaciously convinces the doctor to reveal an alternative remedy—a forbidden ritual contained within an ancient manuscript called the *Kure*.

Although initially rejecting the vile and sinister rite, John realizes, too late, that the ritual is more than a faded promise scrawled on a page of crumbling paper. And as cure quickly becomes curse, the demonic text unleashes a dark power that drives him to consider the unthinkable—a depraved and wicked act requiring the corruption of an innocent soul.

The Kure contains mature content
and is intended for an 18+ audience

The Kure is available in eBook and paperback at
TheKureBook.com

Love Travels Forever

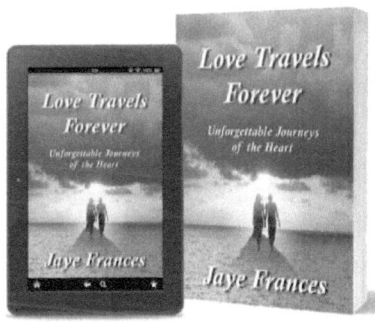

In ***Love Travels Forever***, Jaye Frances captures the reader's heart with an inspiring collection of seventeen stories filled with romance and passion, the hopeful innocence of youth, and a love so strong that it transcends the mortality of life. Here are just a few of the people you'll meet:

Evan and Frankie, a loving couple traveling through life hand-in-hand, are unaware that the shadow of fate is about to tear them apart. Helpless to change their shortened future together, one of them makes a promise—a promise of devotion and courage, honoring a love that surpasses the boundaries of time.

Mark and Janice, the perfect couple with the perfect life, are on the threshold of finally seeing their dreams come true—until an unexpected circumstance changes their lives forever.

Danny, a young soldier fresh out of boot-camp, is desperate to find a way to travel home and marry his sweetheart before being shipped overseas. Stranded in a train station on a three day pass with no hope in sight, Danny meets Wanda, an incredible woman who vows to find a way to bring Danny and his fiance together.

Nora and Georgia are two eight-year-old best friends who share giggles, dolls, and secrets. But when one of them faces sudden danger, the other responds with an unconditional act of love and forges a lifelong bond between them unaffected by fear or prejudice.

So find a quiet spot, get comfy, and grab a box of tissue. You're about to take an unforgettable journey of the heart, to a place where compassion and hope have no limits, and where love continues to travel forever.

Love Travels Forever is available in eBook & paperback at **LoveTravelsForever.com**

Jaye Frances Books are Available in eBook
and Paperback at:

JayeFrancesBooks.com

JayeFrances.com